Praise for
The Chain Letter

"Do we make our own luck, good or bad? A serious question underlies this entertaining friendship story. . . . A lively, enjoyable read."
—*Kirkus Reviews*

"Featuring a cast of well-defined, slightly quirky characters, this novel appeals to all five senses." —*Publishers Weekly*

"Readers will appreciate the story's suspense, humor, and many examples of fine prose." —*School Library Journal*

The Chain Letter

Julie Schumacher

SCHOLASTIC INC.

New York Toronto London Auckland Sydney
Mexico City New Delhi Hong Kong Buenos Aires

No part of this publication may be reproduced, stored in a retrieval system, or transmitted in any form or by any means, electronic, mechanical, photocopying, recording, or otherwise, without written permission of the publisher. For information regarding permission, write to Yearling, an imprint of Random House Children's Books, a division of Random House, Inc., 1745 Broadway, 11th Floor, New York, NY 10019.

ISBN-13: 978-0-439-02007-7
ISBN-10: 0-439-02007-7

Copyright © 2005 by Julie Schumacher. All rights reserved.
Published by Scholastic Inc., 557 Broadway, New York, NY 10012, by arrangement with Yearling, an imprint of Random House Children's Books, a division of Random House, Inc. SCHOLASTIC and associated logos are trademarks and/or registered trademarks of Scholastic Inc.

12 11 10 9 8 7 6 5 4 3 2 1   7 8 9 10 11 12/0

Printed in the U.S.A.   40

First Scholastic printing, January 2007

Acknowledgments

The author wishes to thank Mrs. Holtz's sixth-grade class
(spring 2003) at Groveland Park School, St. Paul, Minnesota,
for their suggestions on an earlier version of this manuscript.

Thanks also to Lisa Bankoff and Charlotte Ruth Simms, for very
valuable advice; and to Jodi Kreitzman, editor extraordinaire.

Thanks to Isabella and Emma and Lawrence Jacobs, for moral
support; and to Allan Amis and James Heyman, who helped with
architectural and scientific questions along the way.

Finally, many thanks to Frederick Schumacher, my father,
for telling me Frank Stockton's story *The Lady, or the Tiger?*
and many other tales.

For my sister, Barb, who told me
I should be a writer when I grew up

Chapter One

Livvie and Joyce got the chain letters in November. They didn't know who had sent them. *Dear friend,* the letters started. *This chain letter has not been broken for fifteen years.*

"Right," Livvie said. "Who do they think they're kidding?"

Joyce was sitting at the kitchen table at Livvie's house, copying the letter onto notebook paper. Her handwriting was short and square, as if every word had been squashed. "The only other chain letters I've ever gotten have been on e-mail," she said. "But a girl I met at camp last summer told me those aren't as powerful. You're supposed to write every single copy by hand. Otherwise it's bad luck."

"It's bad luck just to get a chain letter," Livvie said. "They're a waste of time. Besides, you think everything is bad luck." She opened the refrigerator. She wanted

1

something sweet and hot—maybe a warm brownie with hot fudge and nuts and whipped cream—but her mother had some unexplainable bias against chocolate. Livvie couldn't remember what it was.

"I don't think everything is bad luck," Joyce said. "Just some things."

"Black cats," Livvie said, staring into the refrigerator. "Ladders. The number thirteen. Opening an umbrella indoors."

"And mice," Joyce said. "Mice are bad luck. Most people don't know that." She tore another piece of paper out of her notebook. "Also worms when it isn't raining. When it's raining I think they're all right."

"It's weird that we both got these letters on the same day," Livvie said. They had walked home from school together, stopping first at Joyce's house, where the mail carrier had been stuffing the metal box full of catalogs and bills. Joyce had found her letter in the middle of the stack and brought it with her. A second, identical letter had been waiting for Livvie, at Livvie's house.

"I wonder why they're typed—and not signed," Joyce said. She finished her sixth handwritten copy and began on the seventh. "Who do you think they're from?"

Lazily and without enthusiasm, Livvie looked at her envelope. The postmark was blurry, and there was no return address. "It looks like somebody dropped mine in a snowbank." She looked over Joyce's shoulder. "I hate the way these letters always try to make you feel guilty. *Don't break the chain! This letter began one hun-*

dred thousand years ago when it was scratched into stone by cavemen! You will be a very bad, bad person if you don't send it to all your friends!"

"Better to send it to your friends than bring all that bad luck onto yourself," Joyce said. "I'm almost finished. Only three left." She had taken off her glasses, and now she was leaning so close to the table that the tip of her nose almost touched the letter.

"Well, hurry up," Livvie said. "I'm hungry, and there's nothing good to eat around here." Livvie's mother wouldn't get home from work for another hour and a half. She was a physical therapist and worked with disabled kids, and she didn't have a lot of sympathy for people who complained about a lack of snack food. "I'm reminded every day," she told Livvie at least once a week, "how incredibly fortunate both of us are."

"When are you going to copy yours?" Joyce asked. "I think you really are supposed to do it the same day you get the letter."

"No way," Livvie said. The few times she had been suckered into taking part in a chain letter, she had been told that she would soon be receiving dollar bills in the mail. First a few, trickling in, and then bucketsful! Hundreds! She would be rich! But all she got after forwarding her letters were dirty looks from some of the people she had included in the chain. Her mother, for example. "Take my name off that list," her mother had told her. "I did my time on those horrid things when I was your age. I'm not going to answer them anymore."

Well, Livvie wasn't going to answer them anymore, either—especially if they were supposed to be so much work. "Watch this," she said. When Joyce looked up, Livvie tore her chain letter in half and threw the pieces in the trash beneath the sink.

Joyce stopped scribbling and put on her glasses, as if she couldn't believe what she was seeing. "That's definitely bad luck. Very definitely, Livvie. That's very bad."

"Sure. Whatever. I guess I'm cursed." Livvie studied her friend. It was hard sometimes to know whether to look at the right side of Joyce's face or at the left. Joyce had mismatched eyes: One was bright blue, the other brown. She was like two people combined into one. "There's no one I could have sent it to, anyway," Livvie said. "I can't send it to you or to my mother, and I don't want to send it to anyone at school."

"What about Peter? He likes you."

Livvie scowled. "He doesn't like me *like that*. Besides, Peter wouldn't answer a chain letter." Livvie had known Peter since they were very small. Livvie's mother and Peter's father were both single parents and had been in a babysitting group together. When Livvie was four, she had spent two afternoons a week at Peter's house.

"Just don't blame me when the lousy luck starts coming your way," Joyce said in a singsong. She licked the envelopes and stamped them with Livvie's mother's stamps, then tapped them against the tabletop to straighten them.

Joyce's confidence made Livvie nervous. "How about we just act like we got the one letter and you answered it for both of us?" she asked.

"Nothing doing."

"Fine, then. I don't care." Livvie wiped the eraser crumbs off the table. The letter wasn't really part of a chain anyway. It didn't have any power. It was just a piece of paper delivered to an address in the middle of St. Paul, Minnesota, the city itself just a star on a map. "I'm not superstitious. So I'm not going to worry about it," she said. "Let's go to Krull's."

Krull's was a bakery within walking distance of both their houses, just around the corner from their school. Inside the small shop all the waitresses, as well as the overweight baker, wore white, as if they were working in a hospital rather than a donut store. Livvie left a note on the kitchen table *(Mom, went for a walk around the block with Joyce)*, stuffed her key in her pocket, and shut the door. She tried not to slam it. She and her mother rented half a house—the left half, upstairs and downstairs—and everything that happened on one side caused an echo on the other.

It wasn't cold, for November in Minnesota. There was snow on the ground but it was stained by dogs and car traffic, and Livvie hoped it would soon be covered with a bright new coat. Halfway to Krull's, Joyce stopped at a mailbox. She put her first letter in, then closed the little swinging door, then put the second one in and closed the door, then put the third one in. . . .

"Those aren't very big," Livvie said. "You could put them in all at once."

Joyce shook her head. "I always do it this way. This is the way I have to do it." Open-close, open-close.

Livvie kicked at a rim of icicles on the bottom of the mailbox. "Remind me to tell you, in a dozen years, that you shouldn't get a job at the post office."

Joyce finally finished mailing the letters. "In a dozen years we'll be twenty-four," she said. "And there's no way in the world I'm going to be working at a post office."

"Where are you going to be working?"

"I don't know. Maybe I'll just stay in school forever." Joyce had five brothers, four of them younger. School, she had often told Livvie, was the most peaceful part of her day.

At Krull's they ordered two hot chocolates and a sprinkle donut. The waitress-nurse at the register held out their change, then bobbed her head in the direction of the window. "I think he's been waiting for you," she said. Livvie turned around. It was Peter. He was sitting by himself, and there were two empty chairs at his table. He didn't wave to them or say anything— Peter wasn't much of a talker—but Livvie could tell that he had seen them come in.

"Oh, wonderful," Joyce whispered. "It's your scientist friend."

Livvie knew that Joyce got impatient with Peter,

partly because he had asked her, two years in a row, if he could do a science report on her eyes.

"Come on," Livvie said, collecting their change. "We'll just sit for ten minutes." They carried their cups to Peter's table, Joyce dragging her feet along the way. Livvie pulled out a chair. "So you've been waiting for us?" she asked. "How did you know we were coming?"

Peter looked up and shrugged. "It's winter. I know you get hungry after school. And I know your mother doesn't like to buy chocolate." Peter had black hair, black pointed eyebrows, and rosy cheeks. Livvie often thought he looked like an elf. "Actually I thought you'd be here earlier," he said. "I'm at the end of my second cup."

"And they haven't tried to kick you out?" Joyce asked. The waitresses at Krull's didn't like kids taking up their tables.

"No. I straighten out their stacks of free newspapers when I come in. They let me stay here as long as I want."

"Figures," Joyce said.

Livvie took the lid off her chocolate and smiled. Peter was smart. Although he lived only two blocks away from their neighborhood school, he took a bus to the "gifted" school several miles away. Livvie didn't see why that made any sense, but in St. Paul most of the students were segregated into different groups by first or second grade. There was a school for artistic kids, a school for religious kids, a school for troubled kids, a school for science whizzes, a school for left-handed

7

kids who dyed their hair. . . . Peter had told her that the students at the "gifted" school weren't necessarily smarter. They were the children of people who believed they were smarter. Livvie imagined that the other kids in Peter's classes were the ones who would have sat in the front row at any other school, their hands raised permanently in the air. She pictured them sitting in a single long row, so that everyone could always sit in front.

"Well, we would have been here earlier," Livvie said, "but Joyce was playing with the mailbox."

"I was warding off jinxes," Joyce said. "That isn't playing."

"You ward off jinxes by opening the mail slot ten different times?"

"No, you ward them off by answering chain letters as soon as they're sent to you." Joyce was stirring her chocolate. Livvie knew that she had to stir it clockwise and then counterclockwise before taking a sip. That was Joyce.

"What's a chain letter?" Peter asked.

Joyce rolled her eyes. Livvie had to admit that Peter sometimes seemed to have been born on another planet. He listened only to classical music on the radio and watched the educational channel on TV. Livvie sometimes expected him to ask her, as her grandfather used to before he died, "What are you young people up to these days?"

"It's—well, you get a letter," Livvie explained, "and after you send copies of the letter to half the people you know, you're supposed to get more letters or money or luck from other people on the list."

Peter scratched his head. His short dark hair was veering off in all directions.

"Never mind," Livvie told him. "Joyce can explain it. She's the expert here."

"The point is," Joyce said, sitting up straight in her chair as if suddenly feeling very important, "the whole thing works because at the bottom of the letter, or on the back, there's a list of names and—" She stopped in midsentence, her mouth in an O. "I didn't copy the list. I never copied the list at all. I sent all my letters off without it."

"Are you sure there was a list?" Livvie asked.

"There had to be. It must have been on the back. Otherwise it wouldn't make any sense." She stood up and began patting her coat pockets, looking for the letter. She pulled out a couple of used tissues, a stick of gum, two action figures, and a baby bottle. In Joyce's house, much of the clothing was communal. Joyce's mother said she couldn't be bothered to sort the laundry for so many people, so she just left it in a mountainous pile in her bedroom and let Joyce and her brothers search for whatever they needed. Though Joyce kept her own room fairly neat, she often showed up at school wearing mismatched socks, one glove and one mitten, and a shirt that belonged to her older brother.

"Maybe I left it at your house," Joyce said to Livvie. "But I thought I had it. You made me hurry," she added, grumbling. "I shouldn't have hurried."

"You probably left it on my kitchen table," Livvie said. "I'll bring it to you at school tomorrow."

Joyce continued to search through her pockets while Peter stared into the bottom of his empty cup.

Livvie sighed. "What do you see in there?" she asked Peter. "Is it your fortune?"

"I don't know." Peter passed her the cup. He never seemed to know when she was serious and when she was joking. "I came here to tell you something," he said.

Joyce had taken every speck of lint and dust from her pockets and sprinkled the mess across the table. "Maybe I dropped it," she said. "Do you think I dropped it while we were walking?"

"No, Joyce. Quit it," Livvie said. "The letter's not here. Okay, Peter, what do you want to tell me?"

"It's about my dad." Peter studied his hands. They were terribly clean, the fingernails short and square and perfect. "He wants to ask someone out on a date."

Joyce finally stopped rummaging through her pockets. "Your *dad*? A *date*?" She looked at Livvie. "I mean, oh, sure. I get it. Okay. Your dad."

Livvie had known Peter's father for most of her life. He was a nice person, but he was kind of strange. He had thick gray hair that hung in a ponytail down his back. He worked at home, as some kind of consultant. Peter said he was an auditor, that he helped make sure companies were being honest with their money. He was supposed to be very successful, but he didn't look it. For one thing, he drove a black-and-white-striped car. On the hood and the trunk of it, he had glued about a hundred dolls' heads. They formed a giant ridiculous-looking V on both the front and the back. Then there was his yard, decorated with junk as if every day of the week were Halloween. Peter's dad was weird. And he had bad teeth. It was hard to think of him asking anyone out on a date.

"Who's he going to ask?" Livvie swept Joyce's debris off the edge of the table. "Do you know her?"

Peter nodded.

"Do you like her?"

Peter opened his mouth to answer, but then the waitress came by in her squeaky white shoes and asked if they were finished.

"We've barely started," Joyce said. "My chocolate's still hot." She gestured toward her cup just as Livvie swept a final bit of dust across the table, and somehow the full cup of chocolate cascaded into Livvie's lap.

"Oops," Joyce said. "My mistake. Sorry." She snorted, then bent over and started laughing like a wild hyena.

Twenty seconds later, all three of them were out on the sidewalk, Livvie's pants dripping steadily into her shoes. "I don't see why they threw us out," Livvie said. "I caught all the chocolate before it hit the floor. There's probably nothing left in there to clean up."

"I think there were footprints," Joyce said. "But not very many."

Peter zipped up his jacket. "I've got homework," he said. They headed home.

11

Joyce had to walk on the street side, because she needed to touch every lamppost along the way. "This is how it starts, you know," she said, rapping her knuckle against a metal pole and glancing at Livvie. Peter was several steps in front of them.

"What starts?" Livvie asked.

"The bad luck. From the chain letter. That's why you're covered in chocolate."

"I'm covered in chocolate because you couldn't keep your hands to yourself," Livvie said. "Anyway, it doesn't matter. My pants can be washed. They aren't ruined."

They had come to the top of the street where Peter lived. He waved to them and started down the hill.

"Wait," Livvie said. "You were going to tell us about your dad."

"Never mind," Peter said.

"Come on. Just tell us, and then we'll all be able to go home."

Peter shuffled his feet, and Livvie had the feeling that he had something unfortunate to tell her, something he wished he could just take home with him and forget.

"Come on, it's getting cold out here," Joyce said. She wedged her hands into her armpits. "You said you knew her. Do we know her?"

"Yup. Pretty well," Peter said. "It's Livvie's mom."

Chapter Two

"*Oh, no you don't,*" Livvie said. She was holding on to the collar of Peter's jacket. "You're not doing any homework now. You have to stay here and explain what you mean."

"I think it's pretty clear what he means," Joyce said. "His dad has the hots for your mom."

"He does not," Livvie said. She turned to Peter. "Does he?"

"I saw him write her name down," Peter said. "On a piece of paper."

"So?"

"And I heard him on the phone," Peter added. "He said, 'I'm going to ask Kate McFee. I think she's the one.'"

Livvie laughed at him. "That could mean anything," she said. "Maybe he was going to ask her if she wanted to buy something. Some wrapping paper. Or a cell phone. Or, I don't know, maybe a puppy."

"A puppy?" Joyce asked.

"All I'm saying," Livvie said, "is that just because he wrote her name down somewhere doesn't mean that he—"

Peter had reached into his pocket and unfolded a piece of notebook paper. On the top of the page, in dark ink, was the name *Kate McFee*. And all around it, in red, someone had drawn a circle of hearts, some of them pierced with little arrows.

"Oh oh oh oh oh oh oh," Joyce said. She did a little dance on the sidewalk. "Will you look at that! Wedding bells. You two could end up being related."

"Oh, shut up, Joyce." Livvie's head hurt. She didn't dislike Peter's father. In fact, she knew him well enough to call him Phil. That's what a lot of the kids in the neighborhood called him: Phil Finch. Livvie had liked going to his house for day care when she was little. When she was too young to be embarrassed by his house or his car, or the peculiar things he liked to set outside in his yard.

She turned to Peter. "Okay. So maybe he likes her. There's nothing we can do about that. But you can tell him not to ask her out. Just tell him that she won't want to go."

"Is that really true?" Peter folded up the note and put it back in his pocket.

"Of course it's true. It has to be true. I mean, think about it."

"I hear what she's saying," Joyce said. "Your dad's a good guy, Pete, but he's really weird. I mean seriously weird. In a worldwide weird contest, he'd probably win."

Peter shook his head. "I'm not going to lie to him."

"Why not?"

"Why not?"

"Look, Peter," Livvie said slowly. "I know you like my mom a lot, and I can see why your dad would like her, too, but—"

Peter interrupted her. "I don't like your mom all that much."

"What?"

"She's a nice person," Peter said. "But she's very sloppy."

"So?"

"Your mom *is* a slob, Liv," Joyce said. "Sometimes the dishes in your house aren't washed for a week. I remember once in the summer you had ants all over the place. There were little trails of—"

"Joyce?" Livvie said. "I really wish you'd shut up."

"She has terrible taste in books, too," Peter added. "She buys the stuff they sell at the check-out counter in the grocery store."

"That's what she likes," Livvie said.

Peter nodded, as if Livvie had just offered evidence that her mother wasn't very bright.

"Look, Livvie," Joyce said. "I think Peter's just saying that maybe his dad is kind of weird, but your mom is weird, too. I mean, in a good way. I like her. I like

15

them both. I'm just glad they're not *my* parents, if you know what I mean."

"Great. Fine," Livvie said. "Well, I don't care whether you like my mother or not. She's my mother. And I don't want her going out with Peter's dad."

The three of them stood there for a little while.

"And this has nothing to do with bad luck, Joyce," Livvie said. "Nothing at all."

Joyce tapped another lamppost with her knuckle. She smiled.

Livvie calmed down on the way home. Peter was probably wrong. Of course he was smart, but that didn't necessarily make him right. You could be smart—book smart—but have no common sense. Livvie's mother often said so. There were people she worked with, she said, who had plenty of advanced degrees but turned into idiots every time they opened their mouths.

Besides, Livvie didn't think her mother would *want* to go out with Phil Finch. She and Phil were just friends. Weren't they?

At dinner that night, Livvie cleared her throat and asked her mother if anything interesting had come up that day. Anything new and different. Any news.

"Like what?" Her mother took the lid off a casserole dish and Livvie's heart sank: kidney beans. Livvie poured herself an extra glass of water. She had a talent for swallowing the little blood-colored ovals whole.

"Like—I don't know. Maybe a phone call, or an offer. Something unexpected."

"From one of your teachers?" Her mother was dishing out the casserole.

"No. Stop! That's enough." Livvie held her hand over her plate. "You know I hate beans."

"You have to eat beans if you're a vegetarian."

"But I'm not a vegetarian."

"No, but the person who shops and pays for the food in this house and cooks it is a vegetarian, and that means we're having kidney beans with dinner. I also made corn bread and salad. What did you do after school?"

"Hung out with Joyce." Livvie watched her mother put the serving dish on the counter. Glancing into the sink, she could see the cereal bowls from their breakfast and the crusts from their grilled cheese the night before.

"I had a new patient today," her mother said. "A nine-year-old girl with cystic fibrosis. And she was so cheerful, so silly. She told me a joke, but I don't remember what it was. I tell you, not a week goes by that I don't remind myself of how fortunate you and I are."

Livvie had swallowed five of the little kidneys without tasting their fleshy interiors. She counted the others: twenty-six beans left.

"Oh, and I saw Phil," her mother said. "I ran into him at the gas station. He invited us over for Thanksgiving. Maybe that's the offer you're talking about."

Livvie put down her fork. "What do you mean, he invited us?" she asked.

"For Thanksgiving dinner. At their house." Her mother sliced up the corn bread. It looked very dry, Livvie thought, as if sand had been mixed with the batter. "You and I are alone for the holiday, and Phil and Peter are alone, so we decided to combine forces."

"Why is he inviting us all of a sudden?" Livvie mashed two of the kidneys with the back of her fork. "I thought they always went to Wisconsin for holidays."

Her mother looked surprised. "I don't know. They aren't going this year. It's a friendly gesture."

"So it's just friendly, then," Livvie said. "Just something to do on a holiday with your friends." Ordinarily, she wouldn't have minded going to Peter's for dinner. Phil Finch was a very good cook. He had been widowed for eleven years, since just a few months after Peter was born, and Livvie's parents had been divorced for ten; but Peter's father, unlike Livvie's mother, had learned to cook.

"Well, of course it's friendly," her mother said. "What else would it be other than friendly?"

"I don't know." Livvie tried to butter her corn bread, but it crumbled into tiny pieces. She thought about some of the people her mother had dated. For a month or two her mother had had dinner every Friday night with a poet who carried a walking stick and wore a beret, and she'd gone on at least three dates with a motorcycle salesman who'd said, "Vroom vroom," whenever he answered the phone or came to their door. Livvie didn't understand it. Her mother was pretty. She might be slightly overweight, the middle of her body shaped like an egg, but she had bright friendly blue eyes and a sunny face, and brown wavy hair she was always tucking behind her ears.

Maybe Phil's idea of a date, Livvie thought, would be to have Thanksgiving dinner together and that was it. At least if he was cooking, they would have a good meal. "Do you think they'll have turkey?" she asked.

"Yes, I'm sure Phil will serve turkey. And he said that the idea of vegetarian gravy and stuffing doesn't bother him, so that's no problem."

"Vegetarian gravy," Livvie muttered. "How can gravy be vegetarian?"

"I think we'll bring a dessert or a few side dishes." Her mother glanced toward her recipe box. There were only about a dozen recipe cards in it.

"Just don't bring tofu," Livvie said. "And no beans."

"I could make beans with onions. The kind you like. I could even cook it over there."

"They have a microwave," Livvie warned her. For some reason Livvie didn't understand, her mother detested microwave ovens. She thought that if you stood in front of them long enough, they would rearrange all the atoms inside you.

"I'm sure that lots of people have them," her mother said, wiping her mouth on a napkin. Her tone of voice made Livvie wonder whether she was willing to make some kind of special exception for Phil. Livvie suddenly pictured, as if she had pulled down a screen to look at a movie in her head, a scene in which she and her mother and Peter and his father were holding hands around a microwave and singing songs.

A radio started blaring the news on the other side of the wall. Livvie's mother counted to ten, then banged her fist on the paneling above the salt and pepper shakers. "Darryl!" she shouted.

"Sorry, Kate," said a muffled voice. The volume went down.

"I think Darryl's going deaf," Livvie's mother whispered. "That radio in his kitchen is getting louder and louder."

"If he's deaf, then why are you whispering?" Livvie picked at her meal.

"I worry about him sometimes," her mother said. "He spends a lot of time alone."

Livvie found it hard to imagine why anyone would worry about Darryl. He was a retired firefighter, about six feet tall, with gray hair in a crew cut. His arms were as big as tree trunks. "Darryl probably likes eating by himself." She looked at her mother. "The way we like eating with just the two of us."

Livvie didn't remember when it was "the three of us." Her parents had met on a blind date and gotten married almost immediately, but they had only managed to *stay* married for a couple of years. She watched her mother spear a little cluster of kidney beans with her fork. "Does it make you lonely to be without Dad?" she asked. "Do you wish that the two of you were still together?"

"No." Her mother tucked a curl of hair behind her ear. "Your father's much better off being married to Sharon."

Livvie supposed that was true. Her father lived in Iowa and ran a bed-and-breakfast with his second wife. Livvie spent a month with them every summer. She liked swimming in the creek behind the house and keeping track of the guests in a big black ledger in her father's office. Still, the apartment in St. Paul always felt like home.

"Anyway," her mother said, "we divorced each other for a reason. Your father's a very good person, in his way, but I don't want him under my roof."

Livvie knew that "in his way" meant that her father was very exact and didn't have a sense of humor. "Who *do* you want under your roof?" she asked.

"You." Her mother pointed her fork in Livvie's direction. "I want you under my roof. And Dr. Brown." Dr. Brown was their ancient chestnut-colored cat, so quiet and aloof that Livvie's mother used to say she had to schedule an appointment in order to see him. "I hope you're not trying to tell me that you want to add to the household," her mother said. "You know I'm not buying another animal."

"I know." For several months the year before, Livvie had begged her mother for a guinea pig, a hamster, a gerbil, a dog. Now she decided not to care about another pet, as long as her mother was only going to be friends with Phil.

Her mother looked out the window, where the woman next door was strapping her screaming two-year-old into a stroller. "I'm sorry if it's hard for you sometimes, being the child of a single parent."

"It isn't hard," Livvie said quickly. "I kind of like it."

"You do? Does this mean I should be wondering what you're doing on your own in the afternoons, when your mother isn't home to supervise you?"

"No. You know I'm trustworthy and honest. I'm doing my homework." She glanced at her mother. "Most of the time."

"Well, I'm glad to hear it. More beans?" Her mother lifted the lid from the casserole.

"Maybe later." Livvie still had a little mountain of beans at the edge of her plate. She had managed to bury some of them under her corn bread.

They finished dinner and stacked their plates beside the sink. The phone rang. Livvie's mother picked it up and immediately smiled. "Hi, Phil. We were just talking about you over here. Livvie's excited about the Thanksgiving turkey."

"Right," Livvie said, more to herself than to her mother. She unzipped her backpack and took out her math book. At home, math always looked harder and more complicated than it did in school.

Her mother laughed. "We'll definitely be there. Four o'clock. And thanks—we're looking forward to it."

"We're looking forward to the *food*," Livvie muttered. She took her homework to her room. But even from the opposite end of the apartment, she could still hear her mother laughing and see her winding her arm up in the telephone cord. It was something she did when she was happy, or when she was planning to stay on the phone for a fairly long time.

Chapter Three

"*Did you bring it?*" Joyce asked the next day at school. "Hand it over." She grabbed Livvie's shoulders and whirled her around, checking the outside zipper of her backpack and both of her pockets. "I tried to call you last night but the phone was busy for about eleven hours."

"That was my mom's fault," Livvie said. "Let go of me. What are you—Oh, oops." She had forgotten to look for the chain letter.

"Oops?" Joyce leaned against the row of lockers, facing Livvie, her eyes open wider than Livvie thought eyes were supposed to open. "You forgot?"

"I'm sorry," Livvie said. "But I didn't see it. It would have been on the kitchen table if you left it behind. It wasn't there." She opened her locker, saw that there was no space in it for anything, including her jacket, and closed it again. She had been meaning to clean her locker out.

"I can't believe it." Joyce shook her head. "You said you'd bring it."

"I was going to. But I walked into the house, and my mom was home, so we talked and had dinner, and after I did my homework I took a shower and went to bed. I didn't see it. Really."

"You didn't look for it," Joyce said. "I guess you were waiting for it to jump up and say, 'Yoo-hoo, here I am!'"

"Let's just forget about it," Livvie said. She plugged her ear while Mrs. Winstead, the principal, asked the students over the loudspeaker to please walk quietly to their classrooms. Joyce and Livvie had the same teacher, Ms. Surge, who for unknown reasons made them sit in opposite corners of the room. "We can talk at lunch."

"I need that letter back," Joyce said. "I need you to look for it. And *you* need to look for it. Your luck is terrible already." She chewed on a clump of her hair, something she did when she was nervous.

"I don't need to look for it," Livvie said. "My luck is fine." She didn't mention who her mother had been talking to on the phone.

"Well, mine's not fine. I stubbed my toe this morning and practically ripped off a toenail. Then I broke a plate in the sink and had to clean it up instead of finishing my homework. I can't believe I sent those letters out without the list. That's probably worse than never sending them at all." She pulled a piece of hair from the tip of her tongue. "Do you think your mom might have thrown it away?"

"No. Not on purpose, anyway." Livvie took off her backpack. "Come on, let's go in. We're going to be late."

Joyce didn't budge. She twirled the combination lock on Livvie's locker, and then began twirling the knobs on each of the other lockers in the row. Livvie sighed and went to class without her. She knew that Joyce wouldn't come in until she had spun the lock on every locker in that part of the hall.

At noon they met at their usual table in the center of the lunchroom, Joyce walking from the end of the milk line all the way around the long gray tables even though it was faster to cut through the middle. "What are you having?" she asked when she sat down.

"A sandwich, applesauce, and carrot sticks. The usual. What about you?"

"Soup." Joyce always packed her lunch herself; today she had a stainless steel thermos and a plastic container full of pretzels. She unfolded two napkins, put one of them down as a sort of tablecloth, and set the other on her lap. Then she opened the pretzels, made sure they were all facing the same direction, and uncapped her soup. "So, what happened?"

"What do you mean?" Livvie was struggling with her plastic container of applesauce. The peel-back lid was tightly stuck.

"I mean, you lost your math book. I saw you hunting for it in your desk." She did a perfect imitation of Ms. Surge: *Is there something wrong, Olivia? Are you unprepared for our lesson?*

"I left it at home. I forgot it. So?"

"So . . . Nothing. It's just a coincidence, I guess. Just like the homework I didn't finish."

"Forgetting my math book has nothing to do with chain letters," Livvie said. She tried to bite the foil tab on the plastic container. "I hate these things. I can never get them open." She picked up Joyce's spoon and jabbed at the lid.

"Stop," Joyce said. "Don't poke at it like that; you're going to—"

Abruptly the foil lid gave way, the spoon plunged in, and the applesauce exploded, yellowish gobs of it landing on Livvie's face, her arms, her hair. It was as if someone had put a small firecracker into the middle of the container and lit it just when the top was opened.

"Wow," Joyce said when Livvie looked up, flecks of mashed fruit dripping from her eyebrows onto the table. "I didn't know you could do that with applesauce."

"Can you get me a napkin? Oh, never mind." Livvie picked up her lunch bag and scraped the worst of the mess from her face. Three boys on the opposite side of the table were slapping each other on the back and howling. Joyce told them to be quiet, which only made them more enthusiastic.

"This has nothing to do with bad luck," Livvie said.

Joyce poured her soup neatly from her thermos into its lid. "I didn't say a word."

In music class, after lunch, two girls standing in front of Livvie were whispering and talking. Mr. Kinkead slammed his baton down on the metal stand and pounded through the bleachers, stopping only when his face was about a half inch away from Livvie's. "If you think your voice is so worthwhile, Olivia McFee, you may sing for all of us," he said. He refused to believe that she hadn't been talking, and he made her sing "Blowin' in the Wind" by herself, start to finish. Her voice was small and crooked, and Mr. Kinkead said it sounded as if it had been squeezed from a rusty pipe.

After music class Livvie discovered a wad of gum on the sole of her sneaker. Joyce raised her eyebrows and waited. "Go ahead without me," Livvie said. Because she stopped to clean off the mess, then wash her hands, she was late for gym and had to do jumping jacks while the rest of the class counted.

Joyce didn't look at her.

Everyone lined up for the pommel horse. When it was Livvie's turn, she managed to catch her foot in one of the leather handles while flying full tilt for the pile of mats on the other side. The gym teacher, Mr. Bruggeman, opened his arms. Flailing, Livvie plunged into them. She knocked Mr. Bruggeman flat on the mat, so that he gasped for breath for several minutes after sitting up. Some of the other girls in class laughed so hard Livvie thought they might have to be hospitalized.

In the locker room, Livvie found Joyce in front of the sink, combing her tangled hair with her fingers. "All right," Livvie said. "You win. I'm ready to start looking for that letter."

Unfortunately, the trash had already been taken out at Livvie's. A new white plastic bag, clean and empty, filled the bin under the sink. Livvie and Joyce looked through the recycling, just in case, and through the stack of mail—at least a week's worth—by the phone. They looked through Livvie's room, which was fairly messy, and through her mother's, which was even worse. The letter was gone. "We could look through the garbage out in the alley," Joyce suggested.

"No way. My mom empties the litter box just before she takes out the trash. And there's probably a dozen bags out there."

They decided to walk to Joyce's to see if one of the envelopes had found its way into Joyce's backpack and then into her house. They looked through the kitchen and through Joyce's room and searched for the clothes that Joyce had worn the day before, sifting through a mountain of dirty laundry that included more clothing, Livvie thought, than her mother probably washed in a year.

They found seven dollars in change and wrinkled bills, which Joyce held behind her back while she shouted up the stairs: "Mom? What about pocket money?"

"As long as you're washing things while you're down there," her mother shouted back, "you can keep what you find."

Joyce split the money with Livvie and began to separate the dark clothes from the light. "Turn the washer on, would you?" she asked.

Livvie stared at the machine, in a corner of the cinder block basement. "I don't know how."

"What?" Joyce had gathered up a giant armload of shirts and underwear and socks.

"How do you turn it on?"

"Haven't you ever done laundry?" Joyce looked almost impressed. "What—do you have the servants do it for you?"

"My mom always does it," Livvie said, staring at the knobs on the washer. "Besides, we don't have this much. We're only two people."

Joyce showed Livvie how to use the machine, and then they went upstairs and searched through Joyce's schoolbooks, through her shoes, and even in the zippered lining of her jacket. All the while, Joyce was handing a bottle to the baby, fixing the antenna above the TV, finding her brother's piano music, and keeping the two cats out of reach of the dog. The noise in the house was an orchestra of sound.

Livvie followed and watched. There were so many things that Joyce knew how to do. She could change a baby's diaper, cook simple dinners on the stove, and cut the grass. At Livvie's, there were no diapers, her mother cooked (for what it was worth), and Darryl took care of the lawn.

"It isn't here," Joyce finally said. Together they flopped down on the couch.

Behind one of the cushions Livvie found a plastic dinosaur, half a harmonica, and a very old carrot. "Maybe you should just call the people you mailed your letters to," she said. "You could ask if any of them got the list and the original letter. You might have put it into one of those envelopes by mistake."

"I don't think so," Joyce said. But she agreed to try. She closed her eyes. "Jeez, I'm tired," she said. Joyce looked different when her eyes were shut—like her own twin sister. "Thanks for helping me look around," she said. "Even if you don't believe in bad luck. Not very much, anyway."

Livvie picked at some dirt beneath her fingernail. "We're going to Peter's for Thanksgiving. His dad called my mom. How many bad-luck points do I get for that?"

"Wow." Joyce opened her eyes and sat up. "Are you kidding? So he really did it. He asked your mother out. He got up the nerve." She pushed her glasses up on her nose, her brown and blue irises magnified through the lenses. "Da dum ta da. Da dum ta da." She started humming a wedding march.

"Oh, cut it out," Livvie said. "We're just going to have dinner. You wouldn't have thought anything about it a week ago."

31

"A week ago everything was different." Joyce elbowed Livvie in the stomach. "Today we're living in a whole new world." This was one of Ms. Surge's favorite expressions. She used it whenever she talked about science or computers.

"Thanks a lot." Livvie pulled her hair away from her face. "It's great to have a friend who's so supportive."

"I'm supportive." Joyce looked wounded. "I'm just trying to get you to see the humor in the situation."

"Okay. Where is it?" Livvie asked. "Where's the humor in the situation?"

Joyce pulled her feet up onto the couch. "All right, let's look at it this way. It might not actually be that bad. We both know that Mr. Finch is strange, but your mother has dated some pretty strange people. Who was that magician she went out with—he came to the door in a red cloak?"

"The Marvelous Adam." Livvie sighed.

"And then there was that swimming pool guy. . . . You said he always smelled like chlorine."

"I know, I know. You aren't making me feel any better."

"Okay. Sorry." Joyce leaned back against the cushions. "Oh, and wasn't there a guy who came to your house on Halloween dressed as a squid?"

"He was an octopus," Livvie said. "Just tell me how many chain letters I have to answer to keep my mom from dating Peter's dad."

"Right. Okay." Joyce nodded. "I'll try to help."

Chapter Four

Peter's house, Livvie thought, was the sort of place that people stared at from their car windows when they drove by. Not because of the house itself—it was an average tan and white stucco—but because of the things Peter's father liked to arrange in their small front yard.

He'd started with a dog when Livvie and Peter were little, because both of them loved dogs but Peter was allergic. So Phil bought a giant stuffed dog and built it a doghouse, and he kept it in the front yard attached to a leash, with a little silvery bowl of water and a sign that read BEWARE: THIS DOG IS FRIENDLY ONLY TO PEOPLE UNDER FOUR FEET TALL.

Later he had added a dinosaur—a six-foot *T. rex*—and then, when the *T. rex* was stolen, a couple of department store mannequins he had discovered in a Dumpster. The dummies reclined in folding lounge

33

in front of the doghouse, and as the seasons changed, Livvie and Peter were allowed to dress them in different clothes. Even though they outgrew the dog and then the mannequins, Phil added to his collection of yard art every year. Once Livvie had walked past his house on her way to school and found dozens of rubber alligators glued to the sidewalk. She had seen glow-in-the-dark geese in metal cages, a giant model of the human heart, and a card table covered with plastic sausage links and artificial cheese.

Most people in the neighborhood had a little plot of grass, and maybe some flowers. In the Finches' yard, there was almost no room for grass to grow.

Now, heading up the sidewalk on Thanksgiving Day with her mother, Livvie noticed that one of the mannequins was dressed in a quilted nightgown and held a plastic turkey on her lap. The giant human heart was propped against a tree. Livvie almost expected to see *Phil and Kate* written across the front of it.

"We won't need to stay very long," she told her mother. "We can just eat, and then go home."

"What would the point of that be?" Her mother rang the bell. "Why not stay home by ourselves and eat dinner alone in our rooms?"

Phil opened the door. For a person with a hundred pieces of plastic in his front yard, he was dressed fairly normally in jeans and a black turtleneck; his gray hair was rubber-banded into a braid. Livvie wondered whether someone her mother's age would think he was handsome. Probably not. Not unless his lips were closed, to cover up his crooked teeth.

"Happy Thanksgiving." Livvie's mother kissed Phil (on the *cheek,* Livvie was relieved to notice), then carried her casserole into the kitchen.

Phil had already opened a bottle of wine, and he handed a glass of it to Livvie's mother. "Re-Pete's in his room. Just bang on the door," he told Livvie. When she and Peter and Joyce were little, Phil had christened them Re-Liv, Re-Pete, and Re-Joyce. He was Re-Phil. Livvie used to regret that her mother's name didn't fit the pattern. Now she was grateful that Re-Kate didn't have any meaning.

Livvie hung around in the kitchen for a while, even though she had been specifically invited to leave. Like the rest of the Finches' house, the kitchen was strange. Phil had built a series of tiny glass windowpanes into the wall between the kitchen and the dining room. They weren't windows that could open and close or let in light; they were just thick pieces of wavy glass—you had to bend over to see through them. And in one corner of the kitchen ceiling, he had cut a hole and inserted a narrow spiral staircase, like a path through a giant seashell. The metal stairs led to what had once been an attic, but now was a second-floor study, Phil's private room.

Livvie sat on the cold metal stair and listened to Phil and her mother talk about the mayor of St. Paul and why he shouldn't be reelected. Finally, because the topic seemed safe as well as boring, she went down to the end of the hall and knocked on the door to Peter's room.

"I'm decent," he said.

"You're what?" She put her ear to the door.

When it opened she almost fell in. "The universe is pale green," Peter said. "If you saw it from far away, it would look like this." He pointed to his computer screen. There was nothing on it—no games, no Internet site—just a flat, soothing color.

"What would it look like from up close?" Livvie asked. She put her face near the screen but saw only a dull reflection of herself: plain brown eyes, ordinary nose, plain straight brown hair. She looked like her father instead of her mother; she had her father's narrow mouth and pointed chin.

"Up close?" Peter looked confused. "I don't know what you mean."

"Never mind. It doesn't matter." Livvie looked around Peter's room. It was perfectly neat, as usual, and the walls were covered floor-to-ceiling with astronomy maps, the night sky forever in front of them. In the old days, she and Peter had played with blocks in this room, and sometimes with dolls. Peter had been nice about that. He had even played Barbies. Most of the heads from his Ken doll collection were now firmly affixed to his father's car. Livvie cleared her throat. "They're drinking wine out there in the kitchen," she said. She meant it as a warning.

"I've got wine in here." Peter pointed at a bottle on his desk.

"Since when does your dad let you drink wine?"

"It's nonalcoholic. Apple juice in a fancy bottle." He poured the fizzy juice into two plastic cups and handed one to Livvie. She had the uncomfortable sensation that she and Peter were double-dating with her mother and Phil. She put the cup down. "When's dinner?"

"Not for a while. My dad forgot about the turkey. He just put it in an hour ago."

"My mom doesn't eat turkey anyway," Livvie said.

Peter shrugged. He asked her what she wanted to do. Did she want to play chess? Monopoly? Password? Risk?

"No." Livvie saw the games neatly lined up on his closet shelves. "You're going to win whatever we play."

Peter didn't bother to disagree with her. "We could go for a walk."

"No." Livvie didn't want to leave their parents alone together. She looked at a map of the solar system above the computer. "You don't want them to like each other, do you?"

Peter looked awkward. Despite what he said about her being a slob, Livvie knew that he had always liked her mother. *"Peter?"*

"I don't know," he said. "My dad works by himself all day. At night it's usually just the two of us. Sometimes he talks to me so much I think I'll go crazy."

"There are lots of people he can talk to if he wants to

talk," Livvie said. "I mean, other than my mom. We could find him someone else."

"Like who?" Peter poured himself a second cup of juice.

Livvie considered the people who probably walked past the Finches' house every day on their way to the drugstore or the coffee shop or the school. Most were under fourteen or married. "Mrs. Long," she said. "Isn't she a widow?"

"Mrs. Long's about seventy," Peter said. "She has grandchildren our age."

"How about that kindergarten teacher—Ms. Pitz?"

"My dad doesn't know her. And she's too short, anyway."

"My mom is short."

"But she doesn't weigh three hundred and fifty pounds."

"What kind of attitude is that?" Livvie asked. "He doesn't like Ms. Pitz because she's heavy?"

"He doesn't know Ms. Pitz," Peter said. "I told you, he works alone all day. He doesn't know very many single people. But he knows your mom."

Livvie studied Peter carefully. "You aren't encouraging him, are you?"

"Encouraging who?" Phil was standing in the doorway, looking amused.

"No one," Livvie said.

"Re-Liv. You're the soul of discretion. I came to tell you that Kate and I are going out for a constitutional around the neighborhood. Do you want to come?"

"You're going for a *what*?" Livvie asked.

"He means a walk. I already asked her," Peter said. "She doesn't."

"Too bad." Phil grinned at Livvie. "Then I guess for a little while we're on our own."

Dinner, when it was finally ready several hours later, was very good: It had been a long time since Livvie had eaten turkey. She ate an entire drumstick and several additional thick slices of white meat on buttered bread, along with mounds of stuffing and potatoes. She even put gravy (Phil had made vegetarian as well as regular) on her peas.

She was sitting happily stunned in front of the wreckage on her plate when Phil turned to her and said, "I hear you got a chain letter."

Livvie had the gravy ladle in her hand. She let go of it, and it clattered into the bowl. "How did you know?"

"Re-Pete told me. Was he not supposed to?"

"More e-mail clutter," Livvie's mother said. "Who was it from?"

"Nobody. It was regular mail. And I didn't answer it," Livvie said.

"Good for you." Her mother smiled at her across the table.

"Why didn't you answer it?" Phil asked. His voice was quiet.

When she was little and spent two afternoons a week

at his house, Livvie had loved the way Phil listened to her. He had a way of paying attention that was deeper and better than other adults. Now the way he was waiting for her to answer made her nervous. "Because it's a waste of time," she said.

"Word on the street is that refusing to answer a chain letter can bring bad luck. Do you believe that?"

"No." Livvie looked at Peter. Her eyes were daggers.

"You know what they say about bad luck." Phil tapped his fingers against the tabletop. "It comes in threes."

Quickly, Livvie tallied up the accidents from the previous week. The exploding applesauce was one. The choir disaster, two. The flattening of Mr. Bruggeman in gym was three. Maybe that was it. Then she remembered the gum and the missing math book. And the hot chocolate. And what about her mother sitting here sipping a glass of wine and smiling happily at Peter's dad?

"What number are you up to?" Phil spoke so softly only Livvie seemed to hear.

"I don't believe in bad luck," Livvie's mother said, putting down her wine. "I think it's just an excuse for not picking yourself up and getting on with life. Bad things happen to everybody. It's all a matter of how you handle them. I see that at work every single day."

"That sounds very Republican," Phil said.

"It shouldn't. I'm a common sense Democrat."

Phil smiled. "Don't you think that some people are luckier than others? People who win the lottery, who inherit a few million dollars from a long-lost relative—"

40

"I think that what matters is human character. Learning to make the right choices with what you're given," Livvie's mother said. "Anyway, so far you're only talking about money. Money's not luck."

"That's true." Phil passed the muffins—they were much better than Livvie's mother's corn bread—around the table. "It isn't the good kind of luck. Not the kind that truly matters."

"What's the kind that truly matters?" Livvie asked, despite herself. She was relieved that the adults weren't reminiscing about the old days, when Peter and Livvie shared a playpen and ran around half naked together in Peter's yard.

"The kind that matters," Phil said, dipping into the artificial gravy (Peter called it the un-gravy), "is the kind that allows two people like Kate McFee and Philip Finch to live near each other, and to have dinner together on a national holiday with their charming children, who have so agreeably decided to remain good friends."

Livvie rolled her eyes.

"Hear! Hear!" Her mother lifted her glass.

"A toast," Phil said. "To Livvie. May future chain letters keep their distance. And may good fortune dog her footsteps wherever she goes."

Later, Peter apologized to Livvie in the kitchen. "I shouldn't have told him about the letter. I didn't think he would bring it up."

"Forget about it." Livvie put her plate on the counter, which looked very empty. Normally, the space right next to the sink was taken up by a glass terrarium inhabited by a pair of oversized geckos. "Where are Howard and Leila?"

"In the basement."

"Your dad moved them?"

Peter scraped their plates and filled the sink with soapy water. Both of them knew that Livvie's mother didn't like reptiles.

"He's trying to make a good impression." Livvie shook her head. She could hear Phil and her mother laughing in the dining room. She bent down and looked through the small panes of glass built into the wall and saw the two of them as if through a kaleidoscope—fractured and multiplied, a dozen miniature pairs of them around the room. "Are we supposed to be doing the dishes?" she asked, turning toward Peter at the sink.

"You don't have to. I can do them. I know how you feel about touching slime."

Gingerly, Livvie picked up the paper napkins and threw them in the trash. She dropped the dirty silverware into the sink. She avoided the turkey platter except to pick a sliver of meat from the carcass.

Upstairs in the study, the phone was ringing. It was Phil's business phone, a separate line. "Should I go answer that?" Livvie asked.

"No," Peter said.

"Don't answer it," Phil called.

Finally the answering machine clicked on, but Livvie couldn't hear whether anyone left a message.

42

"We've been getting a bunch of prank phone calls on the business line," Peter said. "A guy calls us just to yell at my dad and call him names."

"What kind of names?" Livvie asked. "What for?"

Peter was searching for a sponge. "My dad was auditing this company in Minneapolis, and none of the numbers added up. He kept going over and over them and finally he realized that somebody was stealing some of the company's money. He figured out who it was, and now the guy's been fired, and he blames my dad. He thinks my dad lied about the audit."

"You should change your phone number." Livvie pulled another sliver of turkey from the carcass.

"It's not a big deal." Peter mopped the counter. "But my dad doesn't want me answering that phone."

Livvie passed the water glasses to Peter. "You know what I don't understand? Your dad's supposed to be a whiz with money, right?"

Peter nodded. The sleeves of his shirt were wet from the sink.

"Well—" Livvie wasn't sure how to phrase the question. "Why aren't you rich? If he can walk into these giant companies and tell them who's cheating, and then tell them how they can make more money, why isn't he making a lot of money for himself?"

"He likes to work for smaller companies," Peter said. "And he doesn't want to work full-time."

"But he could buy a new house, or fix up this one," Livvie said. *And he could buy a new car,* she thought. *And haul some of that plastic junk out of his yard.*

"I don't think he cares about money," Peter said. "Just like your mom."

The phone upstairs began ringing again. Livvie looked up through the hole in the kitchen ceiling. She used to like thinking of the spiral stairway leading through it as a magic beanstalk breaking through the clouds. She put her foot on the bottom step.

"My dad doesn't want people going up there anymore," Peter said, without turning around.

"Not even you? Why not?"

Peter didn't answer.

Livvie looked up into the darkness above their heads. "If he was my dad, I would want to know why."

"He isn't your dad." Peter pulled the stopper out of the sink.

Even over the noise of the water gurgling down the drain, Livvie could hear their parents laughing and talking in the other room.

Chapter Five

On the way to school on Monday, Joyce asked Livvie if she had suffered from any bad luck over the holiday weekend.

Livvie was sucking on an icicle. "I didn't have any food explode in my face," she said. "And I didn't see any black cats raining down out of the sky. What about you? How was Thanksgiving in South Dakota?"

"It was okay." Joyce shrugged. "Except that my grandfather's getting really old and he can't remember any of our names. He kept calling me Frieda." They walked slowly up the school's front steps and into the building, Joyce studying an index card covered with miniature handwriting. It was her turn to recite a speech in Spanish that afternoon. Livvie had stumbled through her speech already and had gotten what Ms. Surge called "a charitable C."

"Hey, what about dinner with the Finches, though?"

Joyce asked. "Did anything happen between Phil and your mom?"

In the stairwell, two boys were fighting over a calculator. Livvie and Joyce walked around them. "Nope. Nothing happened," Livvie said. "We ate a turkey dinner together, and Peter and I played cards, and then my mom and I walked home. It wasn't as bad as I thought it would be."

Joyce peered over the rim of her glasses. "Huh. I hope you don't think they're going to count *that* as a date."

The early bell rang. Livvie felt it vibrate in the pit of her stomach. "What do you mean? Why wouldn't they count it?"

Joyce took off her backpack and then her jacket. "*Los animales domésticos son el perro, el gato, y el pez.* They won't count it because it doesn't count. It isn't a date if your kids are with you. Has he been calling her? Has he put an *I Love Kate* sign up in his yard?"

"Very funny," Livvie said, thinking about the giant heart that Phil had propped against a tree. She wondered if she should walk past the Finches' house on her way home from school.

"*El perro tiene una cola,*" Joyce said. "I sound like an idiot. Who gives a speech about a dog having a tail?"

Ms. Surge appeared in the doorway across the hall like a bad omen. She clapped her fleshy hands in their direction. "Girls?"

Joyce hung up her jacket and closed her locker. "I mailed a bunch of postcards," she told Livvie. "I asked everyone I sent the chain letter to if they'd gotten the list of other people's names by mistake. But nobody's written back to me yet."

"When did you mail the postcards?"

"Yesterday." Joyce stamped the snow from the bottom of her sneakers. "And don't laugh at me, Livvie. Maybe you think your luck's okay, but mine still stinks. I have a sore throat. It's really killing me."

"So you're getting a cold. That isn't bad luck. That's just . . . being sick."

They ducked under Ms. Surge's outstretched arm and into the classroom. Eva, the sensitive girl, was already crying, and one of the Daniels had managed to pinch his hand in a desk. Drops of blood led across the floor from his seat to Joyce's. He had dripped on the back of Joyce's chair.

"Ms. Surge?" Joyce raised her hand. "I have something unsanitary to report."

"Sit down, Miss Pullman."

Joyce wiped up the drop of blood with a tissue, then turned to Livvie and held up three fingers. Three hours until they were released for lunch.

As soon as the blood had been cleaned from the floor ("Daniel—remove yourself to the nurse's office," Ms. Surge said, "and, Eva, turn off the human fountain, please, *right now*"), Ms. Surge announced that she was canceling math and language studies to concentrate on the sixth-grade project. A sigh of relief went around the room. Half a dozen desks away, Livvie saw Joyce fold her index card and put it in her pocket.

"As I'm sure you know," Ms. Surge said, "our project was delayed because of the weather. But at last it's cold enough. The construction is going to begin very soon."

Every year, the sixth graders at several schools worked together to design or build a project. It was supposed to be educational while raising money for the St. Paul schools. One year the sixth-grade classes had built a playhouse and auctioned it off to the highest bidder. Another year they had designed a city garden, and in the spring and summer they had sold all the flowers and the food that they'd grown. But this year they had come up with the best idea yet. They were going to construct a maze. A snow maze, full size, to be built near the baseball field behind Livvie's school.

Livvie and Joyce had been excited about it at first. Back in September they had talked about being architects or designers, and one weekend at Livvie's house, for fun, they had made drawings of a castlelike structure three stories high. They had drawn turrets and snowy staircases and even elevators made out of ice. They'd included beds with pine-needle pillows, and snow-dog guards at every door.

But then the different committees had been assigned by lottery at school, and Livvie and Joyce had both pulled high numbers out of the hat.

"Finance," Joyce muttered every time someone brought up the subject of the maze. "What kind of committee assignment is that? We might as well just hold a giant bake sale."

Ms. Surge ordered the class to get into their committee groups. She began weaving her way among the desks, stopping here and there to lean over a student, the smell of her perfume following her like a little cloud. Livvie and Joyce huddled together at Livvie's desk. They were supposed to have been working on a business plan. Along with a dozen other students in other classrooms and at other schools, they were supposed to estimate what the maze would cost, and how much they should charge for tickets, so that they would make a profit.

"You told me my language presentation was due today," Joyce whispered.

"It was." Livvie was fumbling through her desk. "Ms. Surge changed her mind."

"Why am I always learning something on the wrong day?" Joyce moaned. "When did she give us *maze homework*? Do you have anything in your desk that looks like finance?"

Ms. Surge glided toward them. Joyce quickly tore a sheet of math problems out of her notebook. "You see, Livvie, if we just charge everyone a thousand dollars . . . ," she said.

Ms. Surge leaned over them, her perfume taking up all the available air around the desk. "That looks like your math homework, Joyce."

Joyce looked down at the sheet of paper. "Wow, look at that," she said. "It is. Livvie, where's our finance

49

notebook? Didn't you have it? Weren't you working on it at home all weekend?"

"Um. I don't remember," Livvie said.

"I'll help her look, Ms. Surge," Joyce said. "It's probably in her desk."

"How considerate of you." Ms. Surge folded her arms. "I'll wait." She smiled and opened the lid of Livvie's desk. The rest of the class was quiet. They were waiting, too, as if for their favorite part of a movie.

"I might have left it—" Livvie began.

"Actually, Ms. Surge, you've caught us," Joyce said. "The truth is that we don't have a finance notebook. Not yet. But that doesn't mean that we haven't been working. We've got a ton of great ideas. You're going to love what we come up with. We're going to *amaze* you."

"I'll brace myself for that experience," Ms. Surge answered. "Have you done any of the background work? Have you done any interviews, for example? Looked at other students' business plans? Done any research?"

"Oh, sure, we did some research," Joyce said. Livvie had closed the desk and put her head down on its wooden surface. She felt as if she were resting her neck on a guillotine. "And I think we have an interview lined up. Don't we, Livvie? With an expert."

"Name?" Ms. Surge asked.

"What?" Joyce chewed on her hair.

"The name of the person you're going to interview. Who is it?"

"Oh, yeah. His name is, um, Finch. Mr. Finch. He lives right near here. He sells stock or something."

"Fine." Ms. Surge wrote the name *Finch* on a piece of paper, then continued to the next group of desks.

Livvie lifted her head off her arms and stared at Joyce. "You have to be kidding," she said.

Joyce shrugged and gestured toward Ms. Surge.

"You're supposed to be helping me avoid him," Livvie whispered.

Joyce waited until Ms. Surge was busy at the other side of the room. "Look," she said. "He doesn't want to go out with *you*. He's after your mother. There's a difference."

"But it's going to make him look good. He'll be helping me with my homework."

"Just don't tell your mother he's doing it. She'll never know."

"He'll tell her."

"He won't. Anyway, I didn't hear you chirping up with any good ideas. We have to interview someone." She folded her math work sheet into the shape of a cootie catcher. "What does your schedule look like this weekend?"

"My schedule?" Livvie asked. "I don't have a schedule. I'll be at home."

"Good. Because I have piano on Saturday at noon, and church on Sunday until eleven, and my aunt and uncle are coming over for Sunday dinner. So. Will you call him and set something up?"

Livvie grimaced.

"All right, *I'll* call him," Joyce said. "I'll ask if he can meet us on Saturday morning. Do I look pale? I need some more cough drops."

"No, you aren't pale. And I'm not going anywhere on Saturday before ten."

"Nine-thirty," Joyce said. "And I'll ask the questions. As long as my throat's okay, you won't have to say anything at all."

It snowed every day of that week, a fine powder trickling almost invisibly from the sky. By Saturday morning thirteen inches covered the ground. Livvie woke up to the sound of scraping: shovels on sidewalks, brushes on windshields, sleds on the hill. It was sunny but cold, the thermometer in the kitchen window exactly at zero. Livvie's mother was walking a crooked circle around the kitchen, the way she always did on weekends before she had her coffee.

Livvie got the orange juice and the butter out of the refrigerator, put two pieces of bread in the toaster, and jiggled the black plastic knob. It always got stuck when she tried to use it. "I hate this stupid toaster," she said.

Her mother pushed the knob down easily with a finger. "You just have to understand how to treat it." She kissed Livvie on the forehead, then hunted through the cabinets for her favorite mug, the one with the polar bears holding hands around the rim. "I was up too late last night," she said, yawning.

"You say that every Saturday." Livvie's mother always stayed up late on Fridays. These were her "mystery nights"; she usually read an entire novel, starting at ten or eleven and finishing five or six hours later. "What were you reading?"

"*Florentine*, by Merrill Coates. It's a Bess James mystery. I love Bess James. She always wears clogs and a long skirt when she's out on a case." She filled her mug with coffee, then sipped from it, squinting as if in pain. "Do you want to go skiing this morning? We could go to the golf course. Or we could go look for a piece of woods."

"I can't," Livvie said. "Anyway, I don't like cross-country skiing. It's too slow."

"It's faster than walking," her mother said. "And cheaper than downhill skiing. Do you have other plans?"

Livvie's toast popped up. "I have homework."

"You can't do it tomorrow?"

"No," she said, even though trudging around on the golf course with her mother sounded better than interviewing Phil. "Joyce and I have to work on our maze assignment. And Joyce said she's busy the rest of the weekend."

Out in the side yard, the two little boys who lived next door were making a snow fort. One of them crawled inside it, like a brightly colored animal disappearing into its burrow.

Livvie's mother handed her the raspberry jelly and poured her some juice. "I think the maze is a great idea," she said. "I heard that the ice blocks are going to be delivered early next week. I wonder how big they are. And how heavy."

"I wouldn't know," Livvie said. "I'm not on the ice-block committee. I'm finance, remember?" She opened the silverware drawer to get a knife and found a card that had once belonged to the Marvelous Adam. Parts of his magic deck surfaced around the house every now and then. Every card was a three of clubs.

"Well, no matter what part of the maze you're working on, I'll be eager to go through it when it's built." Her mother unfolded the morning paper. "I like getting lost. You and I are both good at that. You inherited my terrible sense of direction."

"My sense of direction isn't terrible," Livvie said.

"It's worse than terrible," her mother said. "Which street is just south of us?"

"South?" Livvie bit her lip. North and south always struck her as very abstract. She had to be facing in the right direction—toward the north pole—to understand them. "If I had a compass I could tell you."

Her mother laughed and went back to the paper. "By the way," she said, "since you and Joyce are on the finance committee, I have a suggestion. You should sell coffee and hot chocolate outside the entrance to the maze. That'll bring in more money. And it'll keep your customers happy while they wait."

The doorbell rang downstairs. "Come in!" Livvie yelled. She knew it was Joyce. They heard a stamping of feet, and soon Joyce appeared at the top of the stairs, her glasses white with condensation. "I just made Darryl really mad," she said. "I got snow on your sidewalk after he finished shoveling. Now he's sweeping up every flake with a broom. Hey, breakfast! Can I have a piece of that toast?"

"Darryl just acts like he's mad," Livvie said, handing her some toast with jelly. "Anyway, he likes you. And I think he likes shoveling."

"Joyce, are you hungry? I can make some eggs, if either of you want some," Livvie's mother offered.

Joyce wiped her glasses on her shirt and looked at the clock. "No, thanks. It's almost nine-thirty."

"What happens at nine-thirty?" Livvie's mother asked.

Livvie elbowed Joyce in the ribs.

"Uhf!" Joyce said. "Oh. I mean, I never eat after nine-thirty." She looked at the toast in her hand. "Except for toast."

"What about lunch?"

Livvie was putting on her sweatshirt.

"Well, sure, but lunch is different," Joyce said. "I eat lunch around noon. But I like to have a no-eating period between meals. Nine-thirty to twelve. That usually works best."

Livvie's mother refilled her coffee mug. "Well, feel free to come back at noon and I'll feed you. Where are you going to study? Do you need a ride any-where?"

"No, we'd rather walk." Livvie was pulling on Joyce's sleeve. "Let's go."

Phil had made gingerbread with whipped cream, two enormous pans of it. Livvie knew he liked to cook; still, she wondered if he had thought their whole class was coming.

"It's for Re-Pete's astronomy club," Phil told her. "I'm driving it down there at eleven-thirty. But I made a lot, so that you and Joyce could have some."

"Thanks." Livvie nodded. Almost every Saturday of his life, Peter went to the science museum and talked to people about the stars.

"Yeah, thanks for meeting with us," Joyce said. Despite her recent no-eating policy, she crammed a large piece of gingerbread into her mouth. "Pete's working on the maze, too, isn't he?"

"Yup. So am I," Phil said. "I'm one of the parent volunteers."

"Great. Maybe you can give us extra credit. Just kidding. Can I have some milk?"

Livvie pinched her.

"What?" Joyce squeaked.

Phil poured them some milk, then pulled out two chairs, and they sat down at the kitchen table. "All right," he said. "Where do we start? What do you want to ask me? Do you want me to look over your business plan?"

Livvie had imagined that they would meet upstairs in Phil's study. But then she remembered what Peter had said: Phil didn't want anybody going up there anymore.

"Um, we don't have much of a plan yet," Joyce said. In a grocery bag at their feet, they had three pieces of poster board, two Magic Markers, and a blank notebook. "We probably need to start at the beginning."

"Ah." Phil stood up and got a pad of paper and a pen. At the top of the first page, he wrote the word *snow*. "It might help to start with a list of everything that you have to pay for," he said.

"Snow's free." Joyce added more whipped cream to her gingerbread. "Last time I looked."

"Not the right kind of snow. Not the kind that starts with blocks of ice and bulldozers."

"Oh, that kind. I thought somebody already donated it."

"No, a construction company is going to deliver it for free. But the ice isn't free. You'll need to find out what it costs."

Livvie took the notebook out of the grocery bag, opened it, and wrote *what does ice cost?*

"The bottom layer of the maze is going to be set in place with fairly large ice blocks," Phil said. "But the layers above it will be smaller, and they'll use a mix of ice and snow. And the unused blocks will have to be kept covered, probably with hay, or they'll stick together. That'll cost money, too."

Joyce licked her fingers. "So. Who's going to pay for all that?" she asked.

Phil looked confused. He pulled his hair out of its

ponytail. Livvie wished he would cut it. Why didn't he cut it? It was so long. "Ticket sales," he said. "That's where the money's going to come from. You're going to make money selling tickets to the people who want to go through the maze. Right?"

"Oh. Right." Joyce winked at Livvie, who tried not to groan.

Phil wrote *costs* on his pad of paper. Under it he wrote *tickets, labor, materials.*

"We want to sell coffee and hot chocolate," Livvie said.

"So you *are* awake." Phil smiled. Livvie saw his teeth, all crowded toward the front of his mouth, as if hurrying toward an exit. She nodded and blushed.

Phil added *refreshments* to the list, then crossed off *labor* when Joyce said that 297 kids and their parents and teachers would be doing the building. "Now," he said. "How are you planning to cover your costs?" He looked at Livvie but Joyce answered.

"Tickets," she said.

"But you have to pay for some of these things ahead of time. Like the hot chocolate. You'll need to buy it before the tickets are sold."

"We can sell advance tickets," Livvie said. "Maybe for a discount."

"That means less money," Phil said. "Am I right?"

Joyce reached across the table and cut another slice of gingerbread.

While Livvie doodled in her notebook, Phil talked about capital and profit, investment and risk. Maybe they could print up flyers about the maze and include advertisements from local businesses. What would the flyers cost? What would the businesses have to pay? "All right," he said, a few minutes later, glancing over at Livvie's scribbles. "How much of that was useful or made any sense?"

"Some of it," Livvie said, quickly folding up the page in front of her.

"About five percent," Joyce added. "Is this what you do all day?"

Phil smoothed the hair away from his forehead. "Not entirely. I'm an auditor. Businesses hire me to examine their accounting records, and to make sure that everything matches up."

"And that nobody's cheating," Livvie said.

As if on cue, the phone upstairs in the study started ringing. Phil didn't move to answer it. He put his hair back in its ponytail.

"Okay, then," Joyce said. She wiped her hands on her jeans and stood up. "I guess we got our interview done. Are you ready, Livvie?"

Livvie had been ready but now she wanted to wait, to see if anybody was going to leave a message.

The ringing stopped.

They put on their boots and jackets by the door and thanked Phil for the meeting. On their way home Livvie said, "Somebody's mad at him. At Phil. That's why he doesn't answer his phone."

"What?" Joyce had been staring off into space.

"I haven't told my mom about it, but I could if I

wanted to. I mean, if he asks her out on a date. It wouldn't be lying to say he's in trouble."

"What are you talking about?" Joyce asked.

"Phil. He got somebody fired, and I guess the guy thinks it wasn't fair. He thinks Phil cheated him." Livvie felt the snow crunch under her feet. "Peter told me. Also, he's got some kind of secret up in his study."

"What kind of secret?"

"I don't know." They passed the mailbox where Joyce had mailed her chain letters.

"He didn't have to meet with us," Joyce said. "I think he was pretty nice about it. He made us that ginger-bread."

"And you ate about half of it," Livvie said.

They walked toward Joyce's house, Joyce tapping on every streetlight along the way.

"Maybe Phil's the one who sent us the letters," Livvie said. "Maybe that's why he didn't want us to do the interview upstairs. He's hiding the evidence. He's been sending chain letters all over the country."

"Right," Joyce said. She didn't laugh.

"Hey, did you ever hear from any of those people you sent your postcards to?" Livvie asked. "Did any of them get the list of names by mistake?"

"No," Joyce said. Her blue eye was starting to water from the cold. "None of them got the list. In fact, they never got any letters from me at all."

Chapter Six

"*I can't believe* you still think those letters were stolen," Livvie said. She and Joyce were on their way to school. "Who would steal a chain letter? And how would they steal it out of a mailbox? It doesn't make sense."

They had argued about the letters all weekend. From the ten postcards Joyce had mailed, she had gotten only three replies. One was from her great-aunt, who was practically blind and thought she might have misplaced a chain letter; one was from a cousin who had recently moved to a new address; and the third was from a friend from church, who said she didn't *remember* getting a letter from Joyce, but thought it was possible her little sister could have thrown one away.

"Nobody would care enough about a bunch of chain letters to want to destroy them," Livvie said.

Joyce trudged up the street, breathing into her scarf and saying nothing.

"And you only got three answers," Livvie went on. "You haven't heard from the other seven people. Someone must have gotten one of your letters. They can't all have disappeared."

Joyce shook her head. She mumbled something into her scarf. It sounded like "bears too bleed bees."

"What? I can't understand you," Livvie said.

Joyce stopped in her tracks and unwound the scarf from her face. "I said, I don't care if you don't believe me."

"Oh."

"I don't care that you didn't believe in the chain letter, either. The only thing I care about is that, somehow, I ended up with your bad luck."

It was twelve degrees below zero. Now that they weren't moving, Livvie felt the cold sliding into her backbone, carving a terrible icy path up and down her spine. "Let's keep walking," she said.

But Joyce didn't move. Her boots seemed to be glued to the sidewalk. "That's the part that really kills me, you know? *I* sent the letter on and you didn't. *You* broke the chain but *my* letters got lost—if they weren't stolen. *Your* bad luck has infected *me*."

Livvie stared at her. Up ahead, the crossing guards were leaving their intersection, their bright orange flags whipping behind them as they jogged away. "Bad luck isn't contagious, Joyce," she said. "If you think I infected you with something, maybe you shouldn't spend time with me anymore."

The light at the intersection turned green, then yellow, then red again.

Livvie shivered and looked up the block. She could already picture Ms. Surge, hands on her hips, meeting them at the classroom door. *Ladies? I'm sure you have written excuses with you?* "I'm going to school now, Joyce." She started up the hill.

Behind her, Joyce was inching along, barely managing to put one boot in front of the other. Livvie turned around in time to see her drop her scarf. Livvie sighed and went back to pick it up.

"Do I look pale?" Joyce asked her. "I think I have a fever. My throat is killing me."

If they were going to be five minutes late, Livvie thought, they might as well be ten. Pulling up the sleeve of her jacket, she put her wrist against Joyce's forehead. "I can't feel anything. I'm too cold. But you're kind of sticky. Are you sweating?"

"I don't know." Together they headed toward the corner and the traffic light. Joyce took off her hat and wiped her face. The skin around her eyes looked blotchy and damp.

"Maybe you have frostbite," Livvie said. She tried to remember the warning signs. There was nothing about sweating that she could think of.

Joyce struggled out of her mittens and tried to get a cough drop from her pocket. The cough drop stuck to her finger, then fell in the snow.

A bus rumbled by. Out the back window, several kids made faces at them. Joyce was still fiddling with the box of cough drops. They had just missed the light again.

"Hey, look," Livvie said. Up ahead of them, a row of ice blocks about a hundred feet long gleamed like an unclasped diamond necklace across the baseball field. "The snow maze. It's started. They must have delivered the first layer of blocks last night."

Joyce took off her backpack and set it on the icy sidewalk. "I guess I *am* sweating," she said. "I can't tell if I'm cold or hot."

"I wonder how long it'll take to build it," Livvie said. She covered her nose and mouth with a mitten. Her nostrils felt as if they were freezing together. "Joyce? What are you doing? Are you all right?"

Joyce smiled at Livvie in a lopsided way. She had unzipped her jacket, and now she was clumsily trying to take it off.

"Don't," Livvie said. "You're going to freeze."

Joyce mumbled something that Livvie couldn't hear. And then Joyce's knees folded underneath her, and she fell to the ground.

Livvie wasn't sure where they had come from, but very quickly she and Joyce were surrounded by people. A man in a VW bug had a cell phone, and he rolled down his window and announced that he was dialing 911. A woman got out of a minivan and put her fingers under Joyce's nose and said she was breathing. Someone else took off a coat and folded it under her head like a pillow. When Livvie asked how they had known that she needed help, the woman from the minivan told her they had heard her screaming. Livvie didn't remember that part. She remembered only that she had been standing on the frozen sidewalk, helpless, wishing that Joyce would suddenly wake up.

When the ambulance arrived, its revolving light throwing red and blue stripes across the snow, the people who had stopped to help got back in their cars to give the medics room. Livvie watched the attendants put Joyce on a stretcher. She tried to stay calm while she answered their questions: Yes, this was her friend, and her name was Joyce Pullman, and yes, her mother was probably home. She gave them the Pullmans' phone number. Joyce's face was so pale. When they strapped a mask across her nose and mouth, Livvie thought she saw her eyelids flutter.

They covered Joyce with blankets and packed her away in the ambulance.

"Is that your school, right over there?" one of the medics asked. "Can you get there all right?"

Livvie nodded, her breath steaming.

"Good." The medic patted her shoulder. Then he jumped up front, into the cab, and the ambulance, siren blaring, sped away.

Livvie stood on the corner, suddenly alone. She was at least forty minutes late for school and didn't want to have to explain why. Her hands and feet were frozen, beyond feeling. She thought about going home but remembered seeing her house key, on its artificial rock-candy key chain, hanging on the hook behind the front door.

"Do you know which hospital they took her to?" a voice asked.

Livvie turned around and saw Phil, in a giant down parka with a hood, like a navy blue snowman. "I heard the siren," he said. "I came out to see what the trouble was."

"Oh," Livvie said. "I forgot to ask about the hospital. Or maybe they told me which one it was, but I don't remember." On the ground she saw Joyce's mitten, bright red, like a splotch of blood on the snow.

Phil picked up the mitten. "Let's call and find out, then." He extended a puffy blue arm and Livvie walked toward it, and slowly she let Phil lead her down the street and take her home.

One thing Livvie could say about the Finches' house: Even though it was weird-looking, it was comfortable. The two large couches in the living room sagged in the middle, and the kitchen had all the right kinds of food in it: things like ice cream and marshmallow bars and real peanut butter—not the "natural" kind of peanut butter her mother bought, which always separated into oil on top and nuts on the bottom.

As soon as they walked in the door, Phil fixed her a mug of hot chocolate. He added whipped cream on top, squirting it out of a can like shaving lotion. He handed it to her while he dialed the phone. First he called the school to say that Livvie and Joyce weren't coming in, and then he called Livvie's mother at work and left a message on her voice mail.

"Nobody's home at the Pullmans'," he said. "The ambulance crew must have reached them."

Livvie nodded. She was sitting at the kitchen table, the chocolate cooling in her hands.

"I think I'll use the upstairs phone to call the hospitals," Phil said. "That way I won't tie up the other line in case someone wants to reach us. Are you all right?"

Livvie's nose had begun to itch—a sure sign that she was getting ready to cry. She pinched her nostrils shut with her fingers.

"She may have just fainted," Phil told her. "It could be the flu."

It could be, Livvie thought. On the other hand, maybe it was a stroke or a brain tumor. Or a heart attack. Maybe Joyce was dying, right now. Maybe a surgeon was getting ready to cut her open. Livvie should have answered the chain letter.

"Do you want something to eat?" Phil paused at the bottom of the spiral stairs.

Still pinching her nose tightly shut, Livvie shook her head.

"I could make you a sandwich. Do you still like bologna and mustard and cheese?"

"I'm not hungry."

"I've got Swiss cheese."

Livvie took a deep breath and let go of her nose. "You knew my mom's number at work," she said. "I always have to look it up."

Phil blinked. "I have a good memory for numbers," he said. "I can't forget them even if I want to."

Livvie found a copy of the *Guinness Book of World Records* on the chair beside her. Though her hands were shaking, she began flipping through it. She stopped at a picture of the largest dog in the world. "Joyce thinks I bring her bad luck," she said.

"I thought you didn't believe in bad luck." Phil opened the refrigerator and poured himself a glass of milk. He sprayed the top of it with whipped cream, then added multicolored sprinkles. "You told me you weren't superstitious."

"Maybe I'm not, most of the time. But Joyce is. And she definitely thinks it was my fault that she had a sore throat."

"I'm not sure that Joyce's medical knowledge is very extensive," Phil said. He sat down next to her at the table and added some sprinkles to her cup of hot chocolate.

In the middle of the record book, Livvie saw a photograph of a man lifting a motorcycle over his head. "Weird things happen sometimes," she said. "There are plenty of things in the world that no one understands. Maybe all those things that Joyce does, like tapping on streetlights and turning the knobs on the lockers and not stepping on cracks, are really useful. You even said you believed in bad luck. You said it comes in threes."

"I think I attributed that particular belief to folk-lore," Phil said.

"Joyce could be right, though," Livvie said. "I'm probably some kind of walking hex. I didn't answer the chain letter, and now I'm bad luck to myself and other people. I'll probably end up spreading disaster wherever I go."

"You must be a powerful person, then." Phil stirred his milk and cream and sprinkles. "Most people don't have that kind of control over the fate of the planet."

"It isn't control. What if I can't help it? What if it just happens?" Livvie pinched her nostrils shut again. "What does that taste like?"

"What? This? Do you want some?" Phil offered her his glass but she shook her head. "Like liquid marsh-mallows." He sipped the foamy mixture, then wiped his mouth on his sleeve. "I'm going to call the hospitals now. I'll see what I can find out."

"I guess I'll wait down here by myself," Livvie told him, rubbing her nose.

Again Phil paused on his way up the steps. "I suppose I could use this phone," he said. "I probably won't be on it more than twenty or thirty minutes." He opened the phone book and began to dial. Livvie walked into the living room and looked out the window. Mrs. Long, who did appear to be at least seventy years old, was pushing a grandchild's stroller up the street.

Phil was asking someone whether Joyce Pullman, twelve years old, had been admitted. "Just this morning," he said. "Around nine-thirty, or nine-forty-five.

69

Sure, I can hold." Livvie wandered around the house, trying not to imagine Joyce on an operating table, different parts of her body being removed or replaced. Didn't doctors put pigs' hearts in people sometimes? What about pigs' lungs?

"Thanks anyway," Phil said. He hung up and immediately dialed again. He called at least a dozen numbers while Livvie closed her eyes and made a solemn promise. If Joyce recovered, Livvie would never make fun of her superstitions again. She wouldn't tease her about the chain letter, or about black cats or broken mirrors, or salt thrown over the left shoulder. And Livvie would admit that she had brought this bad luck upon them.

She lay on the couch in the living room and read the *Book of World Records* almost all the way through. Phil brought her a bologna sandwich at noon, with mustard and cheese, the way she liked it. He had tracked Joyce down at a children's hospital, but so far no one could tell him how she was. At two o'clock he was pouring butter over a bowl of popcorn when Mrs. Pullman, for whom he'd left a number of messages, finally called.

"There you are, Livvie, sweetheart," Mrs. Pullman said when Livvie came to the phone. "What a terrible scare. But Joyce is fine. Well, not entirely fine, but it isn't serious, thank goodness. It's been a long day already, I can tell you that."

"What isn't serious?" Livvie could hear Mrs. Pullman corralling several of Joyce's younger siblings. She was always involved in a kind of head count: *two, four, six, yes, everyone's here.*

"Mononucleosis. *Karl, sit down.* The fainting happened, they say, because she was tired. Overworked. They give you children so much homework! I know she complained about her throat, and I gave her some lozenges. . . . Well, in any case, she needs to spend a few weeks in bed—that's the remedy—and get some rest."

"Mono—what?" Livvie tried to imagine a person resting in the Pullmans' house. Even Joyce's mother was always exhausted. "So you're home from the hospital?"

"*Billy, no. Leave the baby alone.* No, we're still here, but we're leaving soon, the doctor says. Joyce wanted me to call you—*No more candy! That's enough!* And I want to thank you, Livvie, very much, for staying with her and keeping your head."

"I'll come visit her. I'll bring her homework."

"That would be wonderful. I'm sure she'll appreciate it." Mrs. Pullman said they would call again later, and then she hung up.

"So it's mono." Phil salted the popcorn. "My brother had it once. He spent half of a summer in bed before they discovered it, and then they told him to go back to bed for the other half."

"But he got well?"

"Oh, sure. Back to his old tedious self. He's a dentist in Rhode Island now. Do you want to call anyone else?"

71

Livvie felt almost light-headed. Joyce wasn't dead. Livvie wasn't going to have to stand at the edge of her grave and explain how she had killed her. "What?" she asked. "Call who?"

Phil had written her mother's work number on a slip of paper, and he was handing it to her.

"Oh. I should have remembered," Livvie said. "It's Monday. My mom's in the children's clinic all day. She won't be back in the office until four o'clock." She dimly remembered a conversation in which her mother had told her that in an emergency Livvie could dial the children's clinic's main number. Of course, the general plan in an emergency was that Livvie should go to the Pullmans', or to Phil's.

"I suppose that explains why she hasn't called us back," Phil said. "I was starting to wonder."

Livvie blushed. For the first time it occurred to her that she could have waited for Mrs. Pullman to call her at home. Phil and Peter had a key to her house. She could have borrowed it. That was also a part of the emergency plan.

They heard the front door close. "Dad?" It was Peter, home from school. "What are you doing here?" he asked, finding Livvie in the kitchen.

Livvie told him about Joyce.

"So you stayed here all day?" Peter took off his coat and draped it over a chair.

"I guess I did." Livvie looked at the clock above the stove: 2:45. "I should be going, though. Sorry I stayed so long. Can I borrow your key?"

"It's on the radiator," Phil said. He was still holding the bowl of popcorn he had made for her.

Livvie put on her jacket, collected her books, and found the key. "I'll bring it back tomorrow. Thanks for having me."

Phil bowed, sweeping off an imaginary hat. "The pleasure was mine."

Chapter Seven

Livvie hated being at school without Joyce. The hours in the classroom dragged by, Ms. Surge droning in a tired voice at the front of the room. She insisted on teaching them the difference between adjectives and adverbs (Livvie had always thought these were two different words for the same thing), when all everyone wanted to discuss was the maze. How heavy were the blocks? Why was the center of the maze supposed to be a secret? When could they stop talking about the parts of speech and go out and *build*?

"It's taking forever to get the foundation finished," Livvie told Joyce. "There are only about ten people working on it. And the rest of the blocks aren't going to be delivered until next week. They're afraid they'll melt if the temperature goes above thirty."

It was Wednesday afternoon, the first time since Joyce had gotten home from the hospital that Mrs. Pullman had allowed Livvie to visit. "The walls are only about two feet high," Livvie told her, "but I think when it's taller it'll seem enormous. I wish you could see it."

Joyce readjusted some of her pillows. She was in bed, wearing gray sweatpants and a T-shirt that said *Bob's Ice Fishing Emporium*. Livvie didn't think she looked very sick.

"Did you bring me my homework?" Joyce asked.

"Yup." Livvie opened her backpack and took out three days' worth of assignments in math, English, geography, and science. "Ms. Surge and your mom and I worked it all out," she said. "I'll come by every morning and pick up whatever you need to turn in, and then I'll come back in the afternoon and bring the new homework. I don't mind doing it."

"All right," Joyce said, accepting the pages that Livvie offered her.

Maybe she does look a little pale, Livvie thought. But that might have been because of her bedroom, which was painted yellow. It was the smallest bedroom Livvie had ever seen, about the size of a closet. The bed and a nightstand took up one side of the room, and a wobbly desk and chair filled the other. Joyce kept all her clothes under the bed, in wooden drawers.

"How much longer until you get better?" Livvie asked. She sat at the foot of Joyce's bed, Joyce's knees between them like two knobby mountains under the covers.

"I don't know. They say I could go back to school half-time after winter break."

"After New Year's?" Livvie was astonished. "You're going to stay in this room by yourself for the next three weeks?"

"I'm not by myself all the time." Joyce looked annoyed.

"But you won't be able to work on the maze," Livvie said. "It'll be done before New Year's. And you and I were signed up together."

"Plenty of people will be around to help with the fort," Joyce said.

"It isn't a fort. It's a maze. They're using ice tongs to put the bottom layers together. And we'll spray the outside walls with water, so they'll freeze."

"Whatever. Would you hand me that soda?" Joyce asked. "I'm supposed to be drinking all the time."

Livvie looked at the glass on the bedside table. It was closer to Joyce than it was to her. She handed it over anyway. Having to stay in bed for three weeks could make anyone crabby. "Joyce," she said. "I want to tell you something. I've been wanting to talk to you."

Joyce accepted the soda and sipped through the long plastic straw. "What?"

Livvie took a deep breath. "I think you were right. About the chain letters. I should have made copies the way you did, and I should have mailed them." She waited. Joyce didn't say anything.

"I even looked for the letter again," Livvie added. "The same day you had to go to the hospital. I tore my entire room apart. My mom thought I was crazy."

"Mm." Joyce was still sipping.

76

Livvie studied the blanket that covered her best friend's knees. "Joyce—are you mad at me? Because if you aren't, I can't tell why you're acting this way."

Joyce lifted an eyebrow. "Why would I be mad?"

To Livvie this sounded like a trick question. She decided not to answer it. "This has to be the end of your string of bad luck," she said. "Maybe, you know, it's like a dose of medicine. You've swallowed it now, so you can check it off the list and get better."

"I'm not *swallowing* anything." Joyce leaned toward Livvie. "Other than soda and juice and soup and Jell-O. I'm starving to death but my throat is still killing me."

"Well, that stinks," Livvie said. "But I can't help it if you aren't—"

"Oh, gross," Joyce interrupted her. "There's a spider. Right there on the wall. Would you kill it for me?"

Livvie turned around and saw the tiny brown creature over her head. She didn't believe in killing spiders. Normally, she would have put it outside, but in Minnesota in December that was almost the same as smashing it with a book. "I'll put it in the trash can." She scooped the spider into the basket under the desk, then moved the basket out into the hall. "Coast is clear. Hey, you aren't wearing your glasses. How can you see a spider without them?"

"Easy." Joyce handed Livvie her soda, and Livvie put it on the nightstand, making a mental note that she should wash her hands. "You get to know what things look like in their blurry versions," Joyce said.

"Everything has two versions—blurry and clear. I know what you look like blurry."

"What do I look like?" Livvie sat down.

Joyce put on her glasses, then took them off. "Your hair is different blurry. It's like a brown ring around your face. And your face is a smudge. An oval. But I can still see your eyebrows. Two blurry lines on the oval smudge, and a brown ring around it—that's your hair. And your shoulders are higher than other people's shoulders. I don't know why."

Mrs. Pullman knocked on the door. "Livvie, you're sweet to visit, but it's getting dark. I should send you home."

"Okay." Livvie zipped up her backpack and looked at Joyce. They had been friends since the second grade. "So you aren't mad at me?"

Joyce was riffling through her homework and didn't answer.

"Joyce?"

"I'm just checking to see that everything's here. Didn't Ms. Surge give you any instructions?"

"Instructions?" Livvie shook her head. "I think she said, 'Here. This is Joyce Pullman's homework. Bring it to her and tell her she has to do it.' "

Joyce yawned. "You aren't very good at being sarcastic."

"I'll try to work on it," Livvie said.

"Good. I'm going to take a nap now. See you tomorrow?"

"Sure. The homework delivery service will stop by at

eight-fifteen." Livvie stood up and lingered in the doorway. "Hey, Joyce? I'm bored half to death in school without you."

"I guess that's your own bad luck," Joyce said, and closed her eyes.

On Thursday at school, Livvie sulked by the window. Chin in hand, she watched the traffic going by outside and wondered who was more unlucky: Joyce, who was at home watching TV and drinking soda in bed, or Livvie, stuck in class without her friend. Livvie wanted her life—both of their lives—to go back to normal. Maybe this was what bad luck really was: a sort of crack in the routine, an opening through which you could fall if you weren't careful.

"I don't think I have everyone's attention yet," Ms. Surge said, tapping a ruler on the edge of her desk. "And it's time to form your committee groups. Committee reports are due next week."

The other kids gradually sorted themselves into little clusters around the room. Livvie stood up and shuffled toward Ms. Surge's desk. "I lost my committee partner," she said. "Is it too late to join another group? Should I just work alone?"

Ms. Surge looked at Livvie as if she had never seen her before. She began sifting through a stack of folders. "Let's see, you're, ah, you are—"

"Livvie," Livvie said. "I'm Olivia McFee."

"I know *who* you are, for heaven's sake. I was

wondering *what*. Are you one of the construction supervisors? The engineers?"

"I'm in finance," Livvie said. "Joyce and I were. But she's going to be sick until after New Year's."

"Well, you need to join another group of financial planners. Let me look." Ms. Surge consulted a list, then asked Livvie to give her some time to "set things up." At the end of the day she gave Livvie a piece of paper. "A student at one of the other schools needs a partner, too. He's a planner. I looked up both of your home addresses and you live very close to each other. Maybe you know him."

Livvie looked at the piece of paper. *Peter Finch.*

There should be a world in which coincidences didn't exist, Livvie thought. A world in which they were illegal. The government wouldn't allow your mother to date the parents of your friends. And it certainly wouldn't allow you to be assigned to a finance committee with a member of a certain family you were trying to avoid. There were almost three hundred kids involved in the snow-maze project; it was just her luck, Livvie thought, that her name had to be attached to Peter's.

"You don't think it's a weird coincidence?" she asked him after school on the phone. She had already dropped off Joyce's homework; Mrs. Pullman had said that Joyce was fast asleep.

"Not really," Peter said. "You lost a partner and I

80

never had one. We live near each other. They matched us up."

"Why didn't you have a partner?"

"For the same reason I'm not president of the student council."

"Oh. I get it." Livvie was ransacking the kitchen cabinets: whole wheat noodles, nonfat cereal, crackers without salt.

Peter asked her when she wanted to work on the project.

Livvie sighed and settled on the crackers. "Never. How about never?"

"I think it should be earlier than that. What are you doing right now? I usually have band after school, but today it was canceled."

"Fine, whatever. Come on over."

"We'll combine our numbers," Peter said.

"What numbers?"

There was a pause. "I thought you interviewed my dad. Did you do any other research? Any analysis?"

"Analysis of what?"

"I'll be there in ten minutes," Peter said. "I'm going to bring you what I've got."

What Peter had were several oversized pieces of graph paper covered with charts and equations and numbers. Livvie flipped through them with her mouth wide open, jaw on her chest.

"These are the projections of profit at one dollar a ticket," Peter said. "And here I've calculated the probable number of ticket purchasers depending on the weather—the snow and the cold. Here are my calculations of—"

"I thought we were just supposed to set a price on the tickets, and print some up."

Peter looked blank. "We're financial planners," he said. "Don't you want to make a profit? Making a profit on the maze is up to us."

"Oh, come on," Livvie said. "Most of the work is already done. The teachers are going to look at what we turn in, and at what the other planners turn in, and then they're going to flip a coin to decide what to charge for admission. They just want us to make up some tickets."

Peter looked down at his paperwork. He seemed to suspect that she might be right. "What are we supposed to hand in, then? We have to be graded for our work on the project."

"I don't know. But Ms. Surge is never going to believe that I did any of that work myself. She knows me too well."

They heard the door open downstairs; a moment later Livvie's mother walked in with two bags of groceries.

"Paella," she said, setting the bags on the table in front of them. "I got out of a meeting early at work, and I suddenly thought, *Paella*. But I'm going to make it without seafood." She began unpacking the bags.

"It's rice, Livvie; you'll like it. Pete can stay if he wants. Hi, Pete. I haven't seen you since Thanksgiving."

Peter waved, dejected. He looked sadly at the work in front of him, now partly covered with cans of cat food for Dr. Brown.

"Don't worry," Livvie said. "You'll hand that in, and you'll get credit for it. You'll get an A. The only hard part is going to be making me look like I had something to do with it."

They helped put away the groceries, and then Livvie's mother gave them apples and lumpy peanut butter for a snack, saying that the paella was going to take a little while. She turned on the radio and dumped a huge assortment of vegetables into the sink.

Livvie convinced Peter to abandon their homework and play a few rounds of double solitaire, followed by spit, which ended up ruining the deck of cards. At six-fifteen there was a knock at the door. "That's probably my dad. I'm supposed to be home now." Peter stood up and reached for his jacket.

"No, you're staying," Livvie's mother said. "I already e-mailed Phil and invited you both."

"E-mail!" Livvie almost shrieked. "Why did you send him an e-mail?"

"Why shouldn't I?" Her mother laughed. "It's the easiest way to reach him." She asked Peter to go downstairs and open the door. A minute later Peter and Phil came up the stairs, Phil striding happily into the kitchen with a loaf of French bread under his arm.

"There's talk of paella in the neighborhood." He

lifted a lid off one of the pots. Livvie knew that within ten minutes her mother would be sitting at the kitchen table and Phil would have taken over the sink, the food, the counters—the entire meal.

"Sorry," Peter whispered. "Maybe if I'd left an hour ago I could have kept him at home. He probably didn't want to eat by himself."

"Forget it," Livvie said. She watched her mother fluff up her hair with her fingers. *Stop smiling,* she thought.

Phil put on an apron that was hanging in the closet, and he and her mother looked at the vegetables in the sink and began to laugh. "Another game of cards?" Peter asked.

They played four more rounds of spit with a new deck of cards and watched half of a movie, and finally it was time for dinner—at eight-fifteen.

The paella—all three hours of it—tasted like rice, Livvie thought. Rice was fine, but usually it cooked in twenty minutes. Carefully, she plucked the vegetables from the center of the small yellow nest on her plate and tried not to think about her mother and Phil getting married, the front lawn of the Finches' house taken up by a giant plastic wedding cake with a bride and groom.

After dinner, Phil insisted on helping with the dishes. He cleaned the counters and the stove and even swept the floor, all while questioning Livvie and Peter about the snow maze. He wanted them to estimate how many hours the maze would take to build, given the shoveling and stacking efforts of two hundred and ninety-seven students. (Two hundred and ninety-six, Livvie thought, without Joyce.)

She left to get a pad of paper in the other room. Phil was talking to her mother about weight and stability and pressure. Livvie looked at the clock. It was too late for visitors. Why didn't her mother just tell them to go home? She headed back into the kitchen, ready to announce that it was a school night and she was very tired, when she saw Phil unrolling a diagram on the wooden table. Peter was tapping a ballpoint pen against his forehead, a series of tiny blue dots gradually appearing between his eyes.

"What is that?" Livvie asked.

Peter and Phil both looked embarrassed. In front of them on the table, Livvie saw a detailed drawing of the maze.

"Where did you get this?" she asked. "I thought we weren't allowed to see a picture of the entire thing."

"You aren't," Phil said. He quickly covered the middle of the drawing with a big yellow sticky note, then smoothed his hand over the rest of the page.

"My dad's the one who drew it," Peter said. "He's the advisor to the architecture committee."

"You drew the maze?" Livvie stared at the paper in front of her. "Can I look at it?"

"Nope. I can show you the edges but not the center. I'm hoping it'll confuse a lot of people." He turned to Peter. "That's the part I'm most proud of. I call it the Lady or the Tiger."

"Why?" Livvie looked at the sticky note in the middle

of the drawing, like a blur in the center of a photograph. She thought about Joyce, without her glasses.

"*The Lady, or the Tiger?* is an old short story," Phil said. "Re-Pete used to like it. The gist of it is that a man who's accused of a crime is sent to an arena, where he has to choose between two different doors. Behind one of the doors is a woman—beautiful of course—and behind the other is a tiger. The point is that choices make most people nervous." He started rolling up the drawing. "They want to have their decisions made for them. But out in the maze, they'll have to choose, knowing that only one choice is right and the other ones will get them into trouble."

"But there's no tiger in the snow maze," Livvie said.

"No. No tiger. But there are three choices in the middle, and two of them are wrong."

"So why can't I see it? Peter's seen it."

"Sorry, Re-Liv."

Livvie's mother was putting away the last of the food. "Don't worry about Livvie," she said. "She doesn't read maps. Is anyone willing to take the trash out?"

"Sure, I'll do it." Phil stood up.

"No, *I'll* do it," Livvie said. "Let *me*." She didn't want Phil doing her mother any more favors.

"I've never seen you so eager to help," her mother said. "Take the whole can outside, would you? I don't want the smell of it in here."

Livvie dragged the plastic trash bin toward the kitchen door.

"Jacket?" her mother asked.

But Livvie didn't bother to put one on. She opened the door and pulled the bin out onto the wooden deck they shared with Darryl. The deck was connected to an outdoor flight of stairs that led to the garbage cans and the alley. This was the stupidest part of having an upstairs kitchen, Livvie thought. There was always something to be carried up or down.

"At least put your shoes on," her mother said. But Livvie didn't want to take the time to find them. The steps were sheltered by the roof most of the way, and if she stuck to the inside her socks wouldn't get wet. She closed the door, then lifted the plastic bag out of the bin, the smell of garbage rising up in the frigid air. Her eyes watered. It was ten below.

She set the empty bin upside down behind her.

Stuck to the bottom of it, glued to an old piece of candy or gum, was half of an envelope. *—ivia McFee* was written across the front. There it was. The chain letter. Or a piece of it. She reached for it but ended up knocking the empty trash bin over, sending it clattering down the stairs.

"Livvie?" Her mother opened the back door. "Are you all right?"

"I'm fine." Livvie turned around and grabbed the bag of trash, intending to run with it down the steps so that she could catch up with the tumbling bin. But she had only managed three steps before she fell, one foot sliding out from underneath her, both hands reaching for the handrail but finding nothing, her knee slamming into a wooden step, the garbage exploding all around her in the starry air. She came to a stop on the lower landing, one foot catching between two boards before ending up awkwardly beneath her, her big toe giving way with a sickening crack. She screamed.

Her mother and Phil and Peter and even Darryl, his silver crew cut glowing in the light from the kitchen windows, appeared on the porch for a frozen second. Then they all thundered toward her as the pain in her toe burst forth, opening and getting larger like a terrible flower. They were brushing the snow out of her hair, picking the garbage off her sweater, and asking what happened and where, where did it hurt?

"The envelope," Livvie gasped. "My foot! No, don't touch it! Oh, it hurts!" And then Darryl picked her up and carried her like a baby, down the last of the back stairs and toward her mother's car.

Chapter Eight

Of course her toe was broken. The big one, on her left foot. On the X-ray that the doctor showed her, she could see a crack running through the middle of the bone like a thin white line. She got an Ace bandage for her elbow, which was bruised, ice for her right knee, and a cast from her left knee to her toe that would have to stay on for six full weeks. Her four little toes wiggled like fat pink prisoners peering out from their plaster home.

The painkiller the doctor gave her made her throw up, so she spent the night on the couch in front of the TV, her foot propped on a pillow and throbbing, her head spinning, an empty grocery bag at her side for when she felt sick. She woke the next morning with a bitter flavor in her mouth, the grind and squeal of the garbage truck interrupting her dreams. The house was still dark. She sat up and opened the blinds and saw two men in hooded jackets lifting the heavy metal cans and dumping their contents into the back of the garbage truck.

The envelope, she thought.

Using both hands, she lifted her leg, with its heavy cast, off the pillow, the blood in her foot immediately pounding like a drum. Awkwardly, she made her way to the kitchen window overlooking the yard. All the garbage was gone. Every orange peel and milk carton and tissue that had exploded down the back steps the night before. Darryl had probably picked it up.

She limped to the cabinet under the sink and pulled out the trash can. There was a new plastic bag inside it. She yanked the bag out and turned the bin over and looked underneath it: nothing. Even the sticky piece of candy or gum was gone.

"Are you revisiting the scene of the crime?" her mother asked. She was standing in the kitchen doorway in her yellow bathrobe, her hair sticking out oddly on one side. "I should think you'd had enough fun with the trash last night."

Livvie sat down. "You're up early," she said.

"I'm not sure I ever went to sleep. I read until two or so, and then I heard you throw up, and then there was a confusing period from three to four when I'm not sure whether I was dreaming or awake, and now it's six-thirty, and I need caffeine." She shuffled over to the sink and started making coffee. "It's still cold out," she said. There was a thin layer of ice on the inside as well as the outside of the window. "How do you feel?"

"My toe hurts. And my leg itches. I can't scratch it." Livvie glanced nervously out the back window.

"Maybe a pencil?" Her mother poured water into the coffeemaker.

"What?"

"A pencil. To scratch. Wouldn't that work?"

"It would be too short," Livvie said. "I don't want it getting lost in there."

"I know: a skewer." Her mother rummaged through the kitchen cabinets until she came up with a sort of metal spear. They had tried to grill vegetables on it once.

Livvie felt the tip—it wasn't sharp—then poked the skewer down inside her cast and scratched a spot on her ankle. Outside the window, the trash truck rumbled away. "I found part of the envelope," she said. "From the chain letter Joyce and I were looking for. I tried to reach it. That's why I fell." She told her mother about losing the letter and about Joyce being upset. "And now it's gone again," she said. "At least, I don't see it anywhere. Would you look around in the yard for me? Pleeeze?" She smiled what she hoped was a winning smile.

Her mother stared at her. "You want me to go out in my bathrobe in this impossible weather to hunt for a piece of trash—a little white envelope in the snow?"

"You could get dressed first," Livvie said.

"What a nice offer." Her mother poured a cup of coffee and looked out the back door while she sipped it. "I'll go look," she said. "But only because I'm afraid you'll try to walk down those stairs yourself while I'm not watching." She went downstairs to get her jacket and boots.

"Go out the kitchen door. Up here," Livvie called. "The letter might be somewhere on the steps."

Her mother clomped up the indoor stairs, pulled up the hood of her jacket, and went out on the deck. Livvie watched her searching around on the landing, her hand on the banister. Her mother walked down the steps, looking carefully left and right, then traced a zigzag pattern through the backyard, in the snow. From the window, Livvie pointed out a few spots near the alley. But eventually she gave up. The yard was small. Her mother had crisscrossed every piece of it.

"I didn't see any envelopes," her mother called from downstairs. Livvie heard her stamping the snow off her feet. "In fact, I didn't see a single piece of any kind of trash. When Darryl cleans up, he really cleans. Fire-fighters are probably trained to be very thorough." Back in the kitchen, her mother shivered, poured another cup of coffee, and looked at Livvie carefully. "You do understand that there's no connection between those chain letters and your broken toe, don't you?" she asked.

Livvie propped her cast on a kitchen chair. "Nothing bad happened to me last night until I saw that envelope," she said, silently adding, *except that you invited Phil to dinner.*

"No, nothing bad happened to you until you walked down a flight of outdoor stairs without any shoes on."

"Well, okay," Livvie said. "Then maybe it's my bad luck that I'm an idiot."

"Being an idiot isn't bad luck; it's lack of planning." Her mother tucked a strand of hair behind Livvie's ear. "I need to go to work, but I'll call you at noon, and I'll come home early. Maybe you can practice getting around on that cast today." The night before, her mother had carried her up the front steps piggyback style. Livvie's legs had dangled close to the ground; she was five foot one, almost as tall as her mother.

"I'll call the school before I go." Her mother looked at the clock. "Oh, and, Livvie. You know I don't want you using the oven or the stove."

Livvie rolled her eyes. Did her mother think she was going to spend the whole day baking? "I won't," she said. "But, Mom, don't you think you should check outside in the big trash cans in the alley—just in case?" She smiled hopefully.

"No, I'm not going to root around in the garbage. And you aren't going to, either."

"Then how am I ever going to find out who sent us that letter?"

"Probably," her mother said, "whenever the person who sent it decides to let you know."

There was nothing on TV that morning but little kids' cartoons. Livvie practiced walking from the living room to the kitchen on her cast, but it made her toe hurt, so she sat down and turned on the computer. She went to the Internet and searched for *luck* but didn't find anything useful. She tried the online encyclopedia, typing in *bad luck,* then clicking on a link for *hexes and curses.* Joyce was right. Lots of people believed in these things. The Pennsylvania Dutch were known to paint colorful hex signs on their barns to ward off spells. And they had discovered that staring too long at another person could bring on a case of the evil eye. Livvie wondered what the Pennsylvania Dutch would think of Joyce's eyes.

She printed out a hex sign and taped it to her bedroom door. Then she printed another five copies, colored them in with colored pencils, pinned one to her backpack, and arranged the others on the covers of her books.

She followed the computer's suggestion that she *also see voodoo.* But a voodoo curse didn't seem as likely: Livvie hadn't noticed any zombies rising out of their graves to follow her around.

She was coloring in the hex sign on her bedroom door (green and orange, just the way it had been on the computer screen) when she heard the phone ring. She didn't bother to answer it. She was sitting on a chair in front of her door, her foot and a row of pencils on a second chair beside her. It was too much trouble to get up. She heard the answering machine click into gear: "You've reached the McFees; leave a message, please." Livvie had asked her mother not to rhyme but her mother liked rhymes.

"Hey, Livvie, it's me." Livvie put down her orange pencil. It was Joyce. "Phil came by this morning to pick up my homework, and Peter told me about your toe. I know you're home, so I'm going to keep talking until you pick up your cane or your crutches or whatever and tap your way over to the phone to talk to me. Don't worry, I can wait."

Livvie lifted her heavy leg off the chair and started down the hall.

"I'll sing you a song while I'm waiting," Joyce said. She started a verse of "Red River Valley," a song both of them had been forced to sing in music class, a song Livvie hated. "For they *saaaay* you are taking the *suu-unshiiiine*—" Joyce was belting it out.

"All right, all right." Livvie finally reached the phone. "You're killing me. Stop."

"I thought that would get you. So what happened?"

"Are you allowed out of bed?"

"Special permission today," Joyce said. "I'm on the couch. So tell me."

Livvie took a breath. "I fell."

"Lots of people fall," Joyce said. "You're going to have to be more specific."

"I fell while I was taking out the trash and I broke my toe. The big one. On my left foot."

There was a pause. "Peter said you yelled out something about an envelope."

Livvie watched as Dr. Brown emerged from under the couch and headed stealthily for his dish. "I did. I saw it," she said. "It was definitely the envelope from the chain letter. I was trying to reach it when I tripped. I could have been killed if the railing had broken."

"Lucky," Joyce said. "Did you get the letter?"

"I almost killed myself, Joyce. So I don't feel very lucky. And no, I didn't get the letter. Darryl picked up all the trash, and it's been hauled away."

"Did you notice anything about the envelope? Anything about the stamp? Or maybe a postmark?"

Dr. Brown took three bites of cat food, looked at Livvie with terror in his eyes, and dashed back underneath the couch. "I didn't see anything," Livvie said. "The only thing I could see was my name. And the weird thing is I feel like I knew the writing." Livvie's heart beat a little faster. "I think it was from someone we know."

"What did it look like?"

Livvie tried to picture the torn piece of envelope on the bottom of the trash can. When she closed her eyes she could almost see it; she felt a shiver of recognition. *That's it,* she thought, an idea lightly clicking into her mind and then disappearing. Out on the deck the night before, she was sure she had known the writing, at least for a second. But then her feet went out from underneath her, and the knowledge was gone.

"Girls' handwriting or boys'?" Joyce asked, impatient.

"I don't know. The only thing I remember is that the letters were small but kind of fat. You know, squat."

"Could you imitate it? On a piece of paper? Why don't you come over here and try?"

"Because I have a cast on my leg, Joyce. I'm not dragging myself over there."

Joyce sighed. "Right. I forgot. How about you imitate the writing a few times until you think it looks good, and I'll send one of my brothers over after school to pick it up?"

"Your brothers would do that?"

"Paulie owes me two dollars," Joyce said. "I'll cancel his debt."

Livvie pulled the morning newspaper toward her and wrote her name. Had it been printed on the envelope, or written in script? She thought it was halfway between. She tried making the letters square, but joining them together. The next time, she spaced them farther apart.

"Getting anywhere?" Joyce was quietly humming "Red River Valley."

"It doesn't look right," Livvie said. "I can almost picture the writing in my head, but I can't make it come out that way on paper."

"Was it somebody from school?" Joyce asked.

"I don't know."

"It has to be, since we both got letters. We'll have to get everybody we know to write your name. Do you think you can do that? Maybe next week?"

"Oh, sure. I'm going to walk around the halls all day asking people to sign my name on a piece of paper."

"Okay, how about this? You can send me a get-well card. Everyone can tell me how sorry they are that I've been sick. They'll sign their names. It's not quite as good as signing *your* name but you still might recognize the writing."

"Too late. We already sent you a card. But Ms. Surge just signed it for everyone. You'll probably get it next week in the mail. Hold on a minute; I have to put my leg up." Livvie pulled a chair toward her.

"How big is the cast?" Joyce asked. "Do your clothes fit over it?"

"Only sweatpants," Livvie said. "My mom's going to cut up a pair of my jeans and sew Velcro on them, so I can take them on and off."

"Are you going to ask people to—Oh, man, that's it! You just ask people to sign your cast. Then you lug your broken self over here to my house and we look at the writing. We'll figure out what reminds you of the envelope. I'm a genius! We'll find out who sent us the letter, and we'll both be faithful to the chain, and we'll reverse our luck. Simple."

Livvie thought this idea over. "All right, fine. I'll get people to write on my leg. Starting Monday."

"No pictures, though," Joyce said. "Tell them they have to write a message. Or maybe a good-luck haiku. Ms. Surge loves haiku."

"Ha-ha," Livvie said.

"Call me when you get them. Hey, and, Livvie?"

"What?" Livvie was scratching her leg again, with the vegetable skewer.

"Sorry I was mean to you before. I'm going nuts over here. Oh, and one more thing."

"Yeah?"

"Use a waterproof pen."

Over the weekend Livvie's mother worked hard to entertain her. They played Scrabble (her mother tried to let her win, but Livvie wouldn't allow it), sang made-up lyrics to lousy songs on the radio, and looked through Livvie's baby book. Livvie had always liked seeing the earlier versions of herself. First came the baby pictures, when her mother and father were still together, her mother in bright, loose clothing, her father rigid and straight beside her, his pants looking pressed. Even in the pictures they seemed like a mismatched pair.

"Why did you get married?" Livvie asked, as her mother turned the page to a picture of Livvie and Peter in a little red wagon, pulled by Phil.

"Why did I get married?" The next photograph was of Livvie and Joyce at the neighborhood playground, on a slide. "I thought I was in love," her mother said. "But I was young. It all happened so fast."

Livvie noticed, not for the first time, that her father disappeared from the baby book by the time she was two. Did he keep his own scrapbook of Livvie's progress and achievements? If he did, Livvie had never seen it. "How can you *think* you're in love?" she asked. "If you're really in love, aren't you supposed to *know* it?"

Her mother taped down a picture that was coming loose. "We didn't know how to talk to each other," she said. "We hadn't known each other very long, and didn't know how important that would be." She smiled. "Your dad's not a talker."

Livvie nodded. Her father hadn't even called to ask about her toe. He knew about it—her mother had sent him an e-mail—but he only called to talk to Livvie on Sundays. He was probably waiting for the next afternoon.

"Both of us did our best, I think." Her mother turned the page and Livvie saw a picture of herself at three, wearing a pointed birthday hat and gnawing on a cupcake. "But maybe love is one of those things you can't really control," her mother said. "Maybe it just happens—or it doesn't." She stood up and stretched. "Enough talk about the mushy stuff," she said. "I've got to pay some bills."

Livvie stayed on the couch with her baby book. Her mother had told her once that she didn't want their photo albums to be *accurate;* she wanted them to show only the happiest moments of their lives, the moments in which they seemed to be content. When they were *lucky,* Livvie thought. Now, flipping through the pages, she noticed how many of the pictures included Phil. Sometimes there was just an arm or a leg she recognized as his; sometimes there was a younger version of his face. Of course, that was because of the shared child care. Still, she pictured her mother holding the camera in front of one eye, framing her life's happiest moments, and smiling at Phil. *Click*. Page after page. Maybe her mother didn't even realize it. There were no photos of any of her boyfriends. Not the Marvelous Adam, or the swimming pool salesman, or the Halloween octopus. Not even one.

Livvie's father called before dinner on Sunday, as expected. Now Livvie told him about her fall, about the ice on the back steps, and about having to scratch inside her cast with a vegetable skewer. Because it involved too much explaining, she didn't tell him about the chain letter.

"I broke my arm when I was your age," her father said. "The difficult thing, I remember, was keeping the cast out of the water. It was summer, and all my friends were swimming and I couldn't go."

"I have to take sponge baths," Livvie said. "When I get more used to the cast I'm going to take real baths but hang my leg over the side of the tub."

They talked about the bed-and-breakfast for a while, and Livvie remembered to ask how Sharon was.

"Fine," her father said. "She's looking forward to seeing you this summer."

"Me too," Livvie said, even though the time she spent with her father and Sharon was always slow and quiet.

Livvie's mother was putting two bowls of vegetarian chili on the table. Livvie could smell the garlic bread. "I have to go, Dad."

"That's fine," he said. "Say hello to your mother."

"I will." She always felt that her father sounded relieved when their Sunday-afternoon calls were over. She knew he loved her, but her mother was right: He wasn't very good at conversation, especially on the phone.

"Take care of that toe," he said.

Livvie told him she would. She hung up and hobbled to the table. "Dad said to say hi."

Her mother cupped her hands around her mouth and shouted, "Hi, Stan! How're you doing?"

There was a muffled bang against the wall. "Sorry, Darryl!"

Livvie sat down and ate three slices of garlic bread, then carefully investigated the chili. She suspected it had tofu in it. One of her mother's missions in life seemed to be to put a little tofu into everything. Then she would happily announce, "You didn't even taste it!"

"By the way," her mother said. "Phil offered to pick you up from school in the afternoons."

"What?" Livvie was poking inside the top of her cast with a serving spoon. "What do you mean, he offered? Why?"

Her mother looked surprised. "Because you can't get very far in that cast, and I won't be home to come and get you. I'll drop you off on my way to work, and he'll pick you up after school at three-thirty. It's a very kind gesture."

"But this is a *walking* cast," Livvie said.

Her mother nodded toward the window, where the thermometer outside the glass registered five below. "It's the coldest December in twenty years. And the sidewalks are icy."

"But what about Joyce?" Livvie plucked a mushroom from the chili and set it on the edge of her bread plate. "I'm supposed to be delivering her homework."

"Talk to Phil. Maybe he wouldn't mind swinging by."

"Right. I'm sure he's dying to drive me all over town."

"I doubt he would mind. Phil likes you. He always has." She refilled Livvie's glass with milk. "Maybe he can even take you Christmas shopping."

"Mom, please. I don't see why—"

"Look at that!" Her mother smiled. "You ate the chili. And I bet you didn't taste the tofu in it at all."

Chapter Nine

Getting people at school to sign her cast wasn't as easy as Livvie had thought it would be. Some people who Livvie was certain would never send her a chain letter—such as Mr. Xiong, the vice principal—wanted to take up a lot of room with their signatures. And some people didn't want to sign, but drew pictures instead.

"Write something," Livvie told Dirk and his twin brother, Karsten. She was sitting in the cafeteria, her leg on a chair, holding out markers to anyone willing to sign. "Write a sentence."

"A sentence?" Karsten appeared not to have heard of such a thing. He pushed the white-blond hair away from his forehead. "What do you mean, a sentence?"

"I don't know. Something that'll bring me good luck. A charm."

Dirk ended up writing, *Break a leg, ha-ha,* but

Karsten just shrugged and walked away, handing his marker to a dancer named Emma, who spilled some potato chips on the cast and quickly scribbled, *Good luck, Livvie. You sure need it.* A boy named Mark, who sat near Livvie in class, said that he doubted her toe was really broken. He wrote, *Get well or else.* And Jennifer Langsdorf (the smartest girl in class, and Ms. Surge's pet) actually invented a quick haiku:

> *Broken toes await*
> *Those who carry the trash can*
> *Down icy back steps.*

Halfway through lunch Livvie realized that she was losing track of who had written what. She tried to make a chart on a piece of paper, but some people had written on the back of the cast or on the heel—words or messages she couldn't see. When the bell rang, a shy fifth grader named Isabella handed Livvie a rabbit's foot. "This is supposed to bring good luck," she said. "You can keep it."

Only two weeks earlier Livvie would have laughed and handed it back. Now she thanked Isabella and hung the white rabbit's foot on her backpack next to the hex sign. When the bell rang, she walked slowly, awkwardly, to class.

Livvie assumed that when school was over Phil would wait for the buses to leave, then pull up in front of the building and wave or honk his horn. But at 3:25 she looked out the classroom window and saw his car in the bus lane—the part of the street that said BUS LANE/NO CARS in enormous letters. Some of the other kids in class saw him, too, and outside the school a small crowd had already gathered; most people had probably never seen a black-and-white-striped station wagon with a hundred dolls' heads glued to its surface. Phil sat with the windows rolled up, reading the paper, oblivious to the attention he was attracting.

Livvie felt all the blood in her body rushing toward her face. She waved her hand frantically in the air and asked Ms. Surge if she could leave early. "It takes me a few extra minutes to get to my locker," she said. "And I don't want to get trampled in the hall."

"Fine, go ahead." Ms. Surge looked tired. For some reason, she often seemed to be exhausted by three o'clock in the afternoon.

As much as was possible with her cast, Livvie hurried out of the building, her coat unzipped, her backpack thumping against her spine. Already the kindergartners were walking hand in hand toward the buses. Breathless, she knocked on the window of Phil's car. He rolled it down. "You aren't allowed to wait here," Livvie said, tugging on the door handle. "This is the bus lane." The doors of the school were flung open; the students began pouring out.

"Do you want me to drive around back?" Phil asked. "You could hobble over there to meet me."

Livvie heard someone behind her say, "Who's the guy in the weird-looking car?"

"No," she said, "just open the door."

"Say please," Phil said, but he unlocked the door and took her backpack while she climbed in.

Livvie stared straight through the windshield and hoped no one would notice her. Luckily, some of the windows were fogging up.

Phil drove slowly out of the bus lane but then stopped and kept the car idling next to the baseball field. "What do you think?" he asked.

Livvie looked out the window at the maze. Its outer walls were almost three feet high. A group of students from one of the other schools had worked on it all day, using the snow and ice like bricks and mortar, snow filling in the cracks between the blocks of ice. *Two hundred and ninety-five students,* Livvie thought. Now she and Joyce were both unable to work on the project. Livvie had stayed indoors and read when it was her class's turn.

"How tall is it supposed to get?" she asked, still looking at the maze.

"Seven or eight feet." Phil waved to a couple of kids who were pointing at his car. He tapped the horn for them; it made a sound like a trumpet. "They love this horn," he said. "I told Pete we'd pick him up, too. He's staying late—he has a geography bee coming up. Do you mind?"

"No," Livvie said, shrinking down in her seat. "But can you pick me up at the side entrance next time? Please?"

"Side entrance it is." Phil hit the horn once more before they drove away.

They picked up Peter at the "gifted" school and then drove to Joyce's house. Livvie told Phil that he could leave her there; she would walk home later.

"No, I don't think so," Phil said. "My contract says I drive you to your house. I can wait for you here." He parked the car.

"You're turning the heater off?" Peter asked from the backseat. "Then I'm going in with Livvie."

"Good idea." Phil took the keys from the ignition. "We'll all go in. Don't worry. I'll hang out exclusively with the adults. There'll be no attempts to cross the age barrier."

"Dad," Peter warned.

Together they walked up the sidewalk and rang the bell. Mrs. Pullman answered, kissing Livvie on the forehead and inviting the three of them to come inside. "Joyce is upstairs," she said. One of Joyce's little brothers shrieked with delight when he saw Phil. All the little kids in the neighborhood liked him.

"There you are," Joyce said when Livvie and Peter knocked at the open door of her bedroom. "Where have you been? Let me see that cast."

It was crowded with the three of them in Joyce's tiny room. Joyce sat on the pillow, Livvie sat at the desk with her leg on the bed, and Peter sat on the floor. Livvie pulled up the leg of her sweatpants. Joyce opened a drawer in the nightstand and took out a magnifying glass.

"Who are you, Sherlock Holmes?" Livvie asked.

Joyce paid no attention. "Put your leg over here," she said. "Who's this? Janet Sauers? She wished you good luck?"

"I told her to. Ow. Don't. I can't turn my leg that way."

Peter asked what was going on, and Joyce filled him in. "Livvie remembers what the handwriting on the chain letter looked like. We're going to match it to everyone's writing back at school."

"How?" Peter asked. "Does Livvie have a sample of the writing?"

"No, I—" Livvie began.

"Yes, in her head she does," Joyce said. "She'll remember the writing when she sees it."

Peter scratched his head. "Then why are *you* looking at the cast, if Livvie's the one who'll remember the writing?"

"Because she can't see the back of her own leg." Joyce put down the magnifying glass. "But maybe we could show it to her in a mirror. Or we could copy the cast at a copy store."

"I can't copy my leg," Livvie told her. "I'd probably break the machine."

"Okay, forget my ideas if you don't like them." Joyce flopped back against the pillows. "Never mind."

Peter unzipped his backpack and took out his homework, spreading twenty or thirty index cards across the floor.

"All right, Mr. Intelligence," Joyce said. "Don't just sit over there and ignore us. What would you do?"

Peter flipped a few of the index cards over. "Ask."

"What do you mean, ask?" Livvie said. "Ask who?"

"Everyone. Anyone at school. Just say, 'Did any of you send me a chain letter?' That seems easier than comparing a lot of signatures with some handwriting you only think you might remember."

"Hm," Joyce said.

Livvie looked at her cast, covered with writing she could barely read. She wished it was clean and white again.

Peter glanced at the hex sign and the rabbit's foot on Livvie's backpack and returned to his homework. The card in front of him, Livvie noticed, read *Tokyo, Kyoto, Nagoya, Kobe, Osaka*. A series of numbers was written neatly underneath. Peter looked up. "If you don't want to ask people about the chain letter one by one, you could carry a sign," he said. "Or pin a sign to your back."

"Right." Livvie laughed. "I'm going to wear a sign all day at school."

Joyce pushed her glasses up on her nose. "That's a good idea. I'd do it."

"You would not," Livvie said. "You're just saying that because you know you can't go to school."

"Livvie, think about it." Joyce leaned toward her. Her breath smelled of cake. "You attacked a gym teacher and nearly killed yourself breaking your toe, and I passed out in the cold and had to go to the hospital. And I'm not even mentioning another topic you don't want to bring up." She nodded meaningfully toward Peter. "We can't afford *not* to find out who sent us that letter. Remember, you said you wished you hadn't broken the chain."

They could hear whooping and shouting coming from the downstairs hall. Phil was probably horsing around with Joyce's brothers. When Livvie was little, he had invented a game called lily pad. He had given her and Peter each a dozen pieces of paper, and they had played a game of tag that allowed them to step only on the pages they could manage to throw down frantically at their feet. Livvie had always liked snatching other players' lily pads from the ground.

"Okay, maybe I wish I hadn't broken the chain," she said. "But why should you get to sit here at home while I make a fool of myself in front of the entire school?"

"I'm not just sitting here," Joyce said. "I'm thinking. Planning."

Peter shuffled his note cards. "You don't seem to be coming up with much," he said.

Joyce's face reddened. "You don't seem to come up with very much, either. You and your dad get all those weird phone calls and you don't even do anything about it."

Peter put down his notes and peered at Livvie.

"Sorry. I told her about them," Livvie confessed, shifting around in her chair. "But I didn't think it was a secret. I just told her how your dad got somebody fired, and now the guy's mad at him."

"He didn't *get somebody fired*." Peter scowled, his elflike eyebrows in a perfect V. "The guy was a thief. He was stealing. My dad figured it out. That's his job."

111

"Did you tell your mom?" Joyce asked.

"No," Livvie said. "I figured she'd just get mad at me for spreading rumors. It might even make her take Phil's side."

"Wait a minute." Peter shook his head. "What do you mean, *my dad's side*? Just because we're getting a bunch of stupid phone calls—"

"So you're still getting them," Livvie said. "You have to admit that it's pretty strange. I mean, why would this guy call so often and be so mad if he really *was* stealing? Wouldn't it make more sense for him to be mad if . . ."

"If what?" Peter was staring at her.

"Well, if your dad, you know . . ." Livvie suddenly wanted to change the subject. "If he might have made a mistake. Or something."

"You want to tell your mother that my dad's dishonest." Peter stood up.

"I didn't say that. But don't you think it's weird that he doesn't let you go upstairs anymore, and—"

Phil chose that moment to appear in the doorway of Joyce's bedroom, blindfolded, with an apple crammed in his mouth. Two of Joyce's brothers, laughing wildly, clutched at his arms.

"I'm ready to leave," Peter said. He stuffed his index cards into his backpack and walked out the door.

"He's awfully sensitive," Joyce said, cleaning her glasses on the bedsheet.

Livvie sighed. "I didn't mean anything by it. But

maybe his dad *did* make a mistake. If he hasn't done anything wrong, why does he want to keep people out of his study?"

"Maybe it's a mess up there." Joyce yawned.

"Ready to go, Livvie?" Phil was calling her from downstairs.

Livvie set her cast on the floor and stood up. "Listen, Joyce," she said. "About school tomorrow. I'm not sure that carrying a sign around all day is going to do any good."

"You don't have to be sure," Joyce said. "Only one of us has to be sure." She rearranged her pillows. "And this time, that one of us is me."

At school the next morning, Livvie stuffed her jacket into her locker, then opened her backpack and stared deeply into it for a little while. She had found a note from Joyce in her jacket pocket: *I would do it for you,* it said. *Don't fail us now!* Livvie reread the note for courage, then reached into her backpack and took out a piece of cardboard on a length of string. She hung the sign around her neck so that it flapped behind her. It read:

> To whoever sent me the chain letter,
> Tell me who you are.
> Give me a second chance.
> I will answer this time.

Livvie had expected to be made fun of, and of course she was. Even Ms. Surge walked around her twice, reading the cardboard. And Livvie found a message in her desk after lunch—ten slips of paper made into a paper chain. In bright red Magic Marker, each slip said *Here is your chain letter* or *Livvie McFee is a nerd*.

Still, the teasing wasn't as severe as it might have been, because most of the sixth graders were busy working on the maze. They were happily moving in and out of the building in packs, snow on their gloves and in their hair. They talked about the maze in the hallways, complaining about the parent supervisors and the hard work, even though Livvie knew they would rather be hauling blocks of snow and ice across the baseball field than be warm in school. Livvie studied the maze from a distance while she waited for Phil at the side door that afternoon. In the fading sunlight, the ice walls glittered like silver.

"Impressive, isn't it?" Phil said.

Livvie hadn't even seen him pull up. She was thinking about how to tell Joyce that the sign hadn't worked, that it had been a pointless exercise in self-humiliation.

"We're about a week behind schedule," Phil said, opening the car door. "But it'll be finished in time for New Year's. Everyone's working hard. I was up there myself for a couple of hours yesterday."

"What does the inside look like?" Livvie asked. Her toe was throbbing, and she was glad to sit down on the cold vinyl seat of the car.

"Full of twists and turns." Phil untangled her seat belt. "And very white. It's hard to describe. You'll have to see it for yourself." He pulled onto the road.

Livvie sometimes wished he wouldn't be so nice to her. "Are we picking Peter up?" she asked.

"Not for an hour. Re-Pete's at band practice. Their holiday concert is Friday night."

Livvie wondered why every school in the state had to have a holiday concert. They were all the same—two Christmas carols, one Hanukkah song, one vague hymn about winter weather, and one song for Kwanzaa. Peter played the French horn. Livvie had heard him. He practiced a lot but wasn't very good. "So are you taking me home, or to Joyce's?"

"Neither. I thought I might take you shopping."

"Shopping," Livvie repeated. "You mean Christmas shopping?" Her mother must have suggested it. "Don't you have work to do?"

"I can always work," Phil said. "But I can't always get up the courage to shop. And shopping is something I hate to do alone. Take pity on me."

Livvie stared at her feet. She and her mother celebrated Christmas, but not in a big or churchy way. They usually decorated a little artificial tree, ate a giant breakfast, exchanged two or three gifts, and then settled in for an entire afternoon of old movies. Her mother said Christmas was a perfect day for videos.

Livvie had already bought her mother a box of salted cashews and a pair of gloves. But maybe she should buy her something else. "All right," she said. "Where do you want to go?"

They drove to a gift shop not far from Peter's school, and Livvie looked at bookmarks and candle holders and lotion and soap. Phil browsed behind her. Livvie limped through the narrow aisles until she saw a pair of blue earrings locked in a small glass case. She knew two things about them right away: They would be perfect for her mother, and they were too expensive.

"They're pretty, aren't they?" Phil asked. The earrings were dark blue stones suspended like tears on a set of gleaming silver wires. "What do you think?"

Livvie turned around. Phil's face was hopeful, and abruptly she understood. He wanted to buy them for her mother. He had brought her here so that she could help him buy her mother a gift. A piece of jewelry. She couldn't believe it.

Phil seemed to be waiting.

"I have to use the bathroom," Livvie said. She stumbled toward the back of the store and shut herself inside the little cubicle. She fumed, stamping her cast against the floor. How could she not have guessed? Why did she have to be such an idiot? She stared into the bowl of the sink and started composing a speech in her head: She knew that her mother wanted Phil to drive her around after school, but she wouldn't be needing his help anymore. Thanks anyway. Her toe was fine. It didn't bother her at all.

She washed her hands and sipped some water from

the tap. What could Phil be thinking? That just because he had helped her with a stupid homework assignment she would help him buy jewelry for her mother? She opened the door of the rest room and marched out. "Phil," she said when he turned around. "I'm not going to need a ride tomorrow."

He was waiting patiently by the door. Livvie wondered whether he had heard her.

"I'm just going to walk from now on," she said, speaking more loudly this time. Did he think that a person with horribly crooked teeth and a plastic heart in his front yard and a hundred doll heads on his car could just—

Livvie stopped in front of the store window. "What happened?"

Through the frosted glass she could see Phil's car. The black and white stripes were still there, but the dolls' heads were missing. Every single one of them. A series of glue rings, like the marks from an octopus's tentacles, crisscrossed the hood.

"I was amazed that you didn't notice earlier," Phil said. "You must have been distracted." He dug his car keys out of his pocket. "I found it like that this morning. Whoever took them also put a crack through the back window. I have to get it replaced." He held the door open for Livvie and they left the store.

"This happened right in front of your house? Last night? While you were home?" Livvie gaped at the car, astonished.

117

"It doesn't matter," Phil said. "I was thinking of welding a birdcage to the roof instead. Some of the dolls were getting moldy. The only one I feel bad about was yours."

Livvie blushed. She usually tried not to look at it, but the largest doll head on the car had once belonged to her. The body of the doll had been cloth, and when it had fallen into a pond somewhere, her mother had said it would have to be thrown away. It was a long time ago, but Livvie still remembered crying and pleading for the doll until Phil offered to mount its head on the front of his car. "It'll be like giving her a great big body," he'd said. "She'll be able to travel. She'll see the world." It was the first thing he had ever glued to his car. And back then, the car had probably been in decent shape. Still, to make her feel better, Phil had glued a plastic six-inch doll head to its hood.

Livvie stared at the vacant strip of metal above the headlights. "This is the same guy, isn't it? The one who's mad at you. The one who yells at you on the phone."

Phil looked surprised; then he nodded and opened her car door and walked quickly around to the driver's side.

"Why would he do that?" Livvie asked. Her anger had softened. "Did you call the police?"

"I called them," Phil said. "They came out this morning to take a look. But I doubt my dolls' heads are high on their list of emergencies. I'm not sure they even considered it real vandalism."

"Well, I think it's terrible." Livvie put on her seat belt. "What are you going to do if you catch him?"

"Ask if I can have my dolls' heads back?"

"I'm being serious," Livvie said.

Phil smiled and put the key into the ignition. "What are you thinking? That I should try to get revenge?" He started the engine. "Maybe you're right. Maybe I'll send him a chain letter in the mail."

Chapter Ten

On Thursday, with only a day and a half left before the beginning of their winter vacation, Ms. Surge handed out the final schedule for the snow maze. As she walked around the room with her sheaf of papers, she explained that parents and teachers were going to continue supervising the student builders over the holiday, so that the maze would be ready for customers on January 1.

"I'm counting on all of you," she said. "I've written your names into the schedule by working around any holiday plans or trips you've told me about." She licked her finger. "But check the schedule to make sure that the times and days I've assigned you are convenient."

"Nothing's convenient," muttered Lawrence, who sat behind Livvie. "That's my dang vacation."

"There will be a sign-in sheet on a table at the baseball field," Ms. Surge went on. "So I will know who showed up to participate and who didn't. You'll notice that I'm on the schedule as well."

Lawrence slouched down in his seat, his sneakers beating out a rhythm against the bottom of Livvie's chair.

"This winter project has been more work than many of us expected. But I think you'll agree that the maze is worth it. Personally, I never expected it to be so . . ." Ms. Surge paused. She looked surprised. "So beautiful," she finished.

No one spoke. Along with most of the other students, Livvie turned her head toward the back of the room. Through the window behind them, the maze was a giant lidless box of ice. It was twenty-five yards long and at least as wide, and with the midday sun shining on it, the glare of the outer walls was almost blinding.

With a click of Ms. Surge's red nails, a schedule arrived on Livvie's desk.

Livvie glanced at it. Joyce wasn't on the schedule, of course; she had been excused because of illness. But Livvie saw her own name in several columns. "Ms. Surge?" She raised her hand. "I'm on the list."

Ms. Surge smiled a narrow smile. "We need everyone's help now, Livvie. I'm sure that's clear. I don't remember that you ever gave me a doctor's note saying you weren't able to participate."

"No." Livvie's head was practically vibrating from the drumming of Lawrence's feet against her chair. "But I have a broken bone. In my body. I have a cast on my leg." It seemed unnecessary to point this out, but Ms. Surge was asking.

"If you have a doctor's note, I'll accept it," Ms. Surge said. "Otherwise, you're on the schedule like everyone else."

As soon as her mother got home that afternoon, Livvie asked her to call Dr. Goodale. "She'll definitely give me a written excuse," Livvie said. "There's no way she's going to want me wandering around in this weather with a broken bone."

Walking through the snow *was* a bit difficult, Livvie had discovered; Phil hadn't picked her up after school, and she'd had to limp the five blocks home on her own.

"You don't need to wander around," her mother told her. But she called Dr. Goodale, talked on the phone for three or four minutes, then laughed and hung up.

"What?" Livvie asked. "Why are you laughing?" She had always liked Dr. Goodale, who had treated her for ear infections and strep throat and fevers since she was three weeks old.

"She wasn't exactly sympathetic." Her mother opened a can of soup and poured it in a pot. Luckily, soup from a can was one of Livvie's favorite dinners. "She told me she spent an entire summer playing tennis with a broken arm. And this weekend she's helping to supervise a wheelchair basketball tournament."

Livvie couldn't believe it. "Our family doctor is going to send me out in subzero weather with a cast on my leg?"

"There are plenty of people in this world who have physical challenges much more serious than yours," her mother said. "Just yesterday I worked with a patient who—"

"Okay, you're right," Livvie said. "I get it."

"Anyway," her mother went on, "Dr. Goodale said you should wear two layers of sweatpants and make sure your toes are thoroughly covered. And she's excited about the snow maze. She wants to come see it when it's finished."

"Great. Maybe I'll be walled up in the middle of it, with my leg frozen solid to the ground." Livvie sat down at the kitchen table to wait for dinner. Her mother handed her the plates and silverware and napkins, and Livvie managed to set the table without getting up. "Mom? We aren't doing anything different for Christmas this year, are we?"

"No. Not unless there's something different that you want to do."

Livvie watched her mother fill two bowls with tomato soup. "So we're not having anyone over for dinner. Or going to anyone else's house. It'll just be the two of us."

"Just you and me," her mother said. "Most people we know are busy on Christmas. Darryl goes to visit his daughter in Chicago, and Phil and Peter are driving to see Peter's grandparents."

Livvie poured herself a glass of milk. "So Peter and Phil will be in Wisconsin. They'll be out of town."

Her mother got the bread and butter and salad from

the counter and sat across from her. "Maybe you can explain something to me," she said, putting her elbows on the table. "Why are you suddenly so concerned about Peter and Phil?"

Livvie froze, a spoonful of soup halfway to her mouth.

"First you didn't seem to want to eat with them on Thanksgiving. Then you were moping around the house about having to work on a committee with Peter, who has been a loyal friend to you since you were in diapers. And why on earth would you be rude to Phil when he's done nothing but help you since you broke your toe? He called me at work this morning to tell me that you asked him not to pick you up at school." Her mother stared at her. One of the things Livvie's mother couldn't stand was unkindness. She believed that everyone in the entire world ought to be kind, every day, to everyone else.

Livvie tried to take a bite of bread, but it seemed to turn to paste in her mouth. "He wanted to buy you a Christmas present," she said.

Her mother looked surprised. "Who did?"

"Phil." Livvie wiped her mouth on her sleeve.

Her mother passed her a napkin. "I don't understand. Why was Phil going to buy me a present?"

"I don't know." Livvie tore the napkin in half, then balled it up and put it in her pocket. "We were at the store, and I was thinking that maybe it was a bad idea, and maybe I should say something to him about it, but then I got distracted because of his car. Somebody broke the back window. They vandalized it."

"Someone broke Phil's car window?"

Livvie sat up a little straighter. "He probably didn't want you to know about it. In case you'd think it wasn't safe for me to get a ride home with him anymore." It wasn't really lying, Livvie thought, to let her mother believe that she didn't want to ride with Phil because somebody had broken his car window.

Her mother shook her head as if to clear it.

"I'm sorry if I was rude to him," Livvie said. "But I can walk home from school. Dr. Goodale would probably approve." She pulled the chickpeas out of her salad. Chickpeas tasted like little balls of dirt. "If you still want the present I guess you could call him," she added. "You could just tell him to go ahead and buy it." She tried to imagine her mother calling Phil and saying, *You know that gift you were going to buy me? I want it. Get out your wallet and drive to the store.*

Livvie's mother was stirring her lettuce around on her plate.

With her mouth full, Livvie said, "I was going to buy you something, too. But then when I got distracted by the car, I didn't. So neither of us bought you anything."

"How nice of both of you." Her mother took a large bite of salad and started laughing and coughing. Livvie stood up, laughing also, and pounded her mother on the back.

"Stop! Enough," her mother gasped. She wiped her eyes. "I'm a little confused by this whole conversation. But if you can manage to get home from school on your own, so be it. You only have one more day before your vacation starts." She coughed again, and Livvie got her some water.

Maybe Phil's gift wouldn't have mattered anyway, Livvie thought. At least her mother didn't seem to want it. They didn't talk about Phil or Peter for the rest of the meal.

That night, they had a snowstorm. It started when Livvie and her mother were washing up after dinner, a few perfect six-pointed flakes falling past the window, and then more and more flakes, until the roofs of cars began disappearing, and headlights were faint white globes moving through the snow. On the news, the forecasters called for three or four inches. It was too cold, they said, for anything more.

But by the time Livvie went to bed, the snow had thickened, and when she woke up in the morning and lifted the shade above her bed, she took one look at the brilliant white world and shut off her alarm. It was the last day before winter break, and she knew, with the snow piled around the house in big round shapes, that there would be no school.

She yawned and sat up in bed when she heard the snowblowers revving their engines. Fountains of snow were rising into the air from the Swenders' driveway down the block. Her mother came into her room carrying a cup of coffee. "I'm going to drive in late today," she said. "I want to wait for the plows."

"How much snow is it?" Livvie asked.

"Over a foot. Fourteen inches, the radio says."

Together they looked at the soft, quiet mounds outside the window. There were no edges or straight lines. The yard looked like a country in a dream, Livvie thought.

"Phil called," her mother said. "He and Peter are coming over at ten-fifteen to pick you up. Phil said he fixed the car window. The snow's too deep for you to walk."

"Walk where? Where am I going?"

"All this new snow. Phil said they need to clear out the maze. He called some of the other parents. They want to get as many people up there as they can."

"But there's no school today," Livvie objected.

"I guess that's the point. Three hundred kids with nothing but time on their hands, and a few willing parents. Maybe some teachers. I'd go with you but I'll be at work." Her mother smiled.

Livvie grabbed her cast with both hands and lifted it out of the covers. "Lucky you."

Phil and Peter showed up just after her mother left for work. Phil was cheerful but Peter was quiet; Livvie assumed he was still angry at her because of what she had said about his dad. They waited in the entryway while Livvie struggled into a pair of her mother's old ski pants. Though they were big everywhere else, they barely fit over the ankle of her cast. By the time she'd gotten them on, she was exhausted.

"What about your foot?" Phil pointed to the single purple ski sock Livvie had managed to pull over her cast.

"I don't know," Livvie said. "Is it very cold out?"

Phil rummaged through a bag of hats and gloves in the bottom of the closet. He ended up putting a plastic bag and a heavy stocking cap over her foot, fixing them to her leg with a rubber band. When he helped her down the front porch steps, Livvie felt a sort of guilty relief at the sight of his car: It looked almost normal without the dolls.

There were about twenty-five people at the maze when they got there. Some were carting buckets full of snow out the entrance. Others were hauling blocks of snow and ice on the other side. Peter immediately jogged off to get a shovel.

"How do we know what we're supposed to be do-ing?" Livvie asked. In her mother's ugly old ski pants and a pom-pom hat rubber-banded to her leg, she felt lumpy and ridiculous.

"Probably report to the crew chief," Phil said. He took her arm and led her toward a cluster of teachers and parents at the edge of the field.

Ten minutes later she was sitting on an icy metal chair,

holding a garden trowel. She was supposed to be filling the chinks between the ice blocks with fresh snow, so that no one going through the maze could peek through the walls. Every half hour or so, someone's mother or father would offer to move her chair for her, and soon she was working inside the maze, away from the wind. She was surprised at how much quieter it was in there. Everyone who walked through the entrance seemed to feel it. When they turned the corner, they lowered their voices, as if entering a library or a church.

In the afternoon, a local pizza shop donated a dozen pizzas. Livvie stumbled out of the maze feeling almost blind and saw the row of card tables in the snow, the lids of the cardboard boxes open and clusters of red-cheeked, hungry people gathered around. She reached for a slice of pepperoni and saw a photographer from the *Pioneer Press* taking pictures. He asked if he could photograph her.

"Yeah, I guess." She posed with her slice of pizza in front of the entrance to the maze, her cast propped on a metal chair. All around her, students were using wheelbarrows and sleds and toboggans to move the blocks of snow. "Will that really be in the paper?" Livvie asked.

The photographer shrugged. He had snow in his beard. "That's up to the editor. It depends on what other news we get today. Are you having fun out here?"

"Um, sure," Livvie said. She told him her name, and he wrote it down on a little notebook he stowed in his jacket.

"I wouldn't have known you were having fun if you hadn't told him," Phil said, coming up behind her. "Are you almost ready to go home?"

Livvie nodded. Out the corner of her eye, she saw Ms. Surge, in a pink one-piece snowsuit and matching hat, at the sign-in table. "How long do you think it'll be before the whole thing's finished?"

"Less than a week, at this rate," Phil said. "And then we'll have a hard time keeping people out of it. People will be paying good money to come through this maze, day and night."

"Who would want to come up here at night?" Livvie asked.

"It won't be my dad," Peter said. He had just handed in his shovel. "He's afraid of the dark. He sleeps with a night-light."

"That's because I need to be able to find my way to the bathroom," Phil said.

Still looking grouchy, Peter said that after sixteen years in the same house, most people would remember where the bathroom was.

"That's okay," Livvie said. "I keep a night-light in my hallway." She was still occasionally afraid of the dark: Darkness gave everything a different shape—almost like snow.

Livvie threw her pizza crust in the trash and followed Phil and Peter to the car, a new group of students and teachers taking their places at the maze.

"When's your next shift?" she asked Peter.

"Tomorrow afternoon." He didn't look at her. "Then we go to Wisconsin."

"So after today I'll be coming up here by myself."

"No, we'll probably be back by Tuesday night," Phil said. "We can drive you." He took Livvie home, getting out of the car and making sure she didn't slip on her way up the steps.

"Is Peter okay?" Livvie asked him. "He seems like he's not in a very good mood."

"Re-Pete? Oh, he'll cheer up." Phil took a small gold box from his jacket pocket. "Merry Christmas. Would you mind putting that under your tree?"

Livvie stared at the box, tied with white ribbon. *Unbelievable,* she thought. He had bought them anyway. He must have driven back to the store on his own. She held out her hand for the box as if it were a bomb. What else could she do?

"Merry Christmas," she said. Out of habit, she checked the mailbox at the front of the house. It was empty. She waved goodbye to Peter and Phil and put her key in the door.

When Livvie was younger she used to wish that she had a big family like Joyce's, so that on Christmas morning all the kids would stampede down the stairs and fight over an enormous pile of gifts. But she didn't wish that anymore. She liked the holiday rituals that she and her mother had created over the past ten years.

As always, they woke up early on Christmas morning, put on their bathrobes and slippers, and met in the kitchen, where her mother made coffee and hot chocolate and heated up the cinnamon buns—two each—that they had ordered especially at Krull's. They toasted the day and then each other, and her mother got out the gold-rimmed china plates and filled them with the cinnamon buns and fresh raspberries, their favorite foods. After they ate, they went for a walk, arm in arm, around the neighborhood, getting cold enough that they deserved another cup of something warm when they came back in.

Then they cleared the table in front of the couch and put on her mother's favorite Mozart tape, louder than usual because Darryl wasn't home. They plugged in a string of colored lights around the window and sat down to open presents. Livvie gave her mother the cashews and the gloves, as well as a picture of the two of them in a wooden frame. Her mother gave her a yellow sweater, a watch, and two CDs, and her father sent her a book and a check for a hundred dollars. *Buy something nice for yourself,* he had written on the card. Livvie knew that he wasn't sure what she liked.

There was only one present left: the small gold box tied up with white ribbon. "Is there a name on it?" her mother asked.

"No." Livvie had thought about hiding the box in the back of a closet, but knew her mother would find that sort of dishonesty upsetting, especially on Christmas. "But I know what it is," she said. "And I know it's for you."

"But there's no card." Her mother, wearing the new gloves Livvie had given her, picked up the present.

"You might as well open it." Livvie picked some raspberry seeds from between her teeth.

Her mother opened the box. There were the earrings, the brilliant blue stones surrounded by silver. "Are these from you, Livvie?" she asked.

"No." Livvie opened one of the CD cases. She knew how the earrings were going to look. She didn't want to watch her mother put them on.

"I don't understand," her mother said.

Livvie pretended that the CD in front of her was the most interesting thing in the world. "I guess Phil bought you a present after all," she said.

Her mother held one of the earrings up to the light.

"You don't really like them," Livvie said. "Do you?"

Her mother put them on, one silver strand and then the other. The blue stones matched her eyes exactly. "I didn't buy anything for him or Peter." She seemed confused.

"Neither did I," Livvie said. "I thought that'd be weird. All of us buying each other something. Wouldn't it be weird?"

Her mother didn't answer.

Livvie lay down among the piles of wrapping paper and ribbon. Maybe she could write Phil a note. She could pretend it was from her mother. *Dear Phil, I don't have the slightest idea why you would want to buy me a Christmas present. . . .*

"Look at this," her mother said. She was turning the Mozart tape over. "I didn't notice it earlier. You're in the paper, Livvie. Look."

Livvie pushed a pile of wrapping paper out of the way and sat up. In the middle of the page her mother was holding were several pictures of the snow maze. In one of them, Livvie sat in the foreground, eating a slice of pizza and resting her cast on a folding chair.

Her mother read the caption. " 'Twelve-year-old Olivia McFee takes a well-deserved lunch break.' Here, you should read the whole story. That's exciting."

Livvie tried to feel excited. She didn't want to let a pair of earrings ruin her holiday. She read the article and ate some cashews while her mother cleaned up. Then the two of them took the pillows off the couch and spent several hours nibbling and watching old movies: Her mother had rented *Roman Holiday* and *Bringing Up Baby,* two black-and-white favorites, and a stack of others. They lay on the floor, wrapped in blankets in front of the TV, and didn't get up except to get more food or use the bathroom. Dr. Brown, in a rare demonstration of holiday friendliness, napped at their feet.

Livvie was rewinding one of the movies when she heard her mother say, "What's this?" She was pointing to the rabbit's foot on Livvie's backpack.

"Oh, it's nothing." Livvie shrugged.

"It isn't nothing. It looks like it used to belong to an

animal. A rabbit. I'm surprised. I thought they'd stopped selling things like this. Don't you think it's cruel?"

Livvie hadn't thought about rabbits' feet actually belonging to rabbits. "I didn't buy it. Somebody gave it to me. It's a charm. You know, like a kind of insurance."

Her mother rubbed the little white foot. "Insurance against what?"

"Anything," Livvie said. "It's for other people as much as it is for me. It's a way of telling them that I'm not going to infect them with my lousy luck." She sighed, thinking about the earrings. "Or at least, I'm going to try to keep all my bad luck to myself."

Her mother frowned. "Livvie, think about what you're saying. You're going to 'infect' people with bad luck? Does that make sense?"

"I don't know. Maybe." Livvie took the tape out of the VCR. "I mean, a lot of things don't make sense. I don't know how the TV works. We put this video in that slot, and all of a sudden we see talking pictures. That doesn't make sense."

"It makes sense to people who understand it," her mother said. "There's a rational explanation. *I* can't perfectly explain how it works, but there are people who can."

"Maybe there are people who can explain how the rabbit's foot works, too. Maybe we just don't know the right people."

Livvie's mother unfastened the little chain from the

backpack and put the rabbit's foot on the table, which made Livvie nervous. "You're a person with a lot of good sense, Olivia McFee," she said. "Remember that." She kissed Livvie's forehead. "Luck isn't something you can count on. *Hard work* you can count on. And using your brain."

"Well, my brain's telling me that I want another piece of pie," Livvie said. "Do you want one?" Deciding that she would reattach the rabbit's foot later, she went into the kitchen and cut a large slice of blueberry pie for her mother, and an even larger slice of chocolate cream for herself. The phone rang, and her mother answered it in the other room. Livvie's father had already called, and so had Joyce. It was probably Phil. Livvie thought about plugging her ears with her fingers. Maybe he wanted to find out how the earrings looked.

Livvie put two cat treats in Dr. Brown's dish as a Christmas present. She ate her pie in the kitchen, waiting for her mother to get off the phone. Finally, she put her empty plate in the sink and went back to the living room, wondering whether jewelry could be returned after it had been worn. "So what did he say?" she asked.

Her mother turned around, the lights in the window blinking behind her. "That was my aunt Caroline," she said. "From Arizona. She was calling to say that my uncle died. He had a heart attack this morning."

"Your uncle Jim?" Livvie had met him but didn't know him very well. She remembered him as a giant red-faced man who had taken her fishing when she was five.

"She wants me to help her. To go down there for the funeral," her mother said. "I can't believe it. He was only sixty."

"Should I go with you?" Livvie asked. She looked for the rabbit's foot on the table.

"No, I don't think so," her mother said. "It might be easier if we found a way for you to stay here." She tucked her hair behind her ears. "I can't believe it," she repeated. Phil's earrings dangled by her neck like tiny blue flames.

Chapter Eleven

The way for Livvie to stay home turned out to be Phil. Livvie argued that she should be allowed to stay with Joyce, but there was the mononucleosis, first of all, and Joyce's parents had a very full house already, with a couple of grandparents sleeping on the fold-out couch. Phil and Peter, on the other hand, had plenty of room.

"Don't you think it's inappropriate for me to stay at a boy's house?" Livvie asked. Her mother had already talked to Phil, who had *just happened to call* from Wisconsin. Supposedly, he wanted to know if Livvie could turn on the warming light above the lizards' terrarium. He had forgotten to ask the family next door to do it.

"No, I don't think it's inappropriate. Not unless you're planning to do something silly while you're there. I wouldn't walk to the bathroom stark naked, for example."

"I never walk to the bathroom naked."

"Good. So it won't be a problem." Her mother was packing. She was leaving the next morning. Peter and Phil were driving back early and would be home sometime after noon.

"You don't think it's awkward?" Livvie uncapped one of her mother's lipsticks. "Your asking Phil for a favor like this?"

Her mother took the lipstick away from her and put it in her suitcase. "No, I don't." She wasn't wearing the earrings anymore. Livvie wondered if she was going to bring them to Arizona. "He knows I would do the same for him at a moment's notice."

"Great." Livvie flopped down on her mother's bed and asked, not for the first time, why she couldn't just stay at home by herself. "Darryl's probably coming home tomorrow, too. And he's right on the other side of the wall."

"That's not close enough. And Darryl hasn't offered to keep an eye on you. I'd ask your father, but I don't know how I'd get you down to Iowa. Anyway, this is one of his busiest seasons." Her mother shoved a book and a hair dryer into the suitcase and zipped it shut. "I'll only be gone for a few days. I'll be back before New Year's. We can walk through the maze together then."

Livvie rolled over on her mother's bed and groaned. She had planned on a very lazy winter break: a few walks to Krull's, a few hours of reading, a few hours of talking about nothing with Joyce. Now, day after day, she would be at the mercy of her mother's would-be boyfriend. And she would be living with two people who loved weird projects, who probably woke up at four in the morning to take apart the toaster and see how it worked.

"Do you want to watch another movie?" her mother asked.

"No. I'm not in the mood anymore." Livvie didn't even remember what they'd already watched. They unplugged the colored lights and put the pies in the freezer. Dr. Brown crept under the couch in the living room. Another Christmas was done.

Early the next morning, Livvie's mother made breakfast and double-checked that Livvie had a key to the house. "Just bring in the mail and the newspaper every day and feed Dr. Brown," she said. "Otherwise I expect you to be at Peter's. They should be back from Wisconsin at about one or two. They'll call when they get here. And if by any chance they get delayed, you can wait with Joyce. I've already talked to Mrs. Pullman."

"All right," Livvie said. She wanted to point out that Mrs. Pullman probably let Joyce stay by herself overnight, but she could see that her mother was anxious. Her mother didn't like airports or flying or planes. The one time they had been on a flight together, Livvie had found the experience dizzying and wonderful. She had especially loved eating lunch thirty thousand feet above the earth on a plastic tray. But now, because of the bad-luck bubble that seemed to surround her, she was anxious, too.

"I'm sorry about Uncle Jim," she said.

"Thanks. So am I. He was a good person." Her mother looked at her watch. They were waiting by the door downstairs. A cab was coming any minute.

"Would you take something with you if I asked you to?" Livvie touched her mother's sleeve.

"I guess that depends. What is it?"

Livvie held up the horseshoe she had gotten at camp when she was nine. She had ransacked her desk and her dresser to find it.

"Oh, Livvie." Out in the street, a cab slowed down and pulled over. "We can't protect each other that way," her mother said. "I wish we could. It would be so easy. But you and I—we just don't have that kind of power. Nobody does."

"So you're saying we're helpless," Livvie said. She had a lump in her throat. The distance between Minnesota and Arizona seemed enormous.

"Not helpless," her mother said. The cab honked its horn. "We're very resourceful when we need to be. But some things are . . . well, they're out of our hands. And it's better that way." She took the horseshoe and set it on the steps behind her. "Knowing you love me and want to protect me is enough. I don't need any good-luck charms."

The cab honked again.

"Give me a kiss," her mother said. "Have fun while I'm gone. No superstitions."

"Call me," Livvie said.

"I will." Her mother started toward the cab. On her suitcase, the white rabbit's foot hung from the strap Livvie had used to attach it. It was barely visible against the snow.

Livvie spent the day reading and watching TV. Phil and Peter got back later than they'd thought they would, Phil pulling into the driveway only about an hour before dinner. He carried her duffel bag to the car.

"Sorry about your uncle," Peter said when she got in.

"Thanks," Livvie said. She was glad that he didn't seem to be angry at her anymore. That was one of the good things about Peter: He never stayed angry very long.

At the Finches' house, Phil tossed Livvie's bag into Peter's room. "I'm bumping Re-Pete out onto the couch," he said. "You can sleep in here."

"No, that's okay," Livvie said. "I'd rather have the couch. Really. I like couches." She didn't want to sleep in Peter's bed, beneath his blankets. She hadn't slept at the Finches' since her afternoon naps on the rug, when she was three or four.

For dinner, Phil made hamburgers with bacon and cheese, one of Livvie's favorites. Howard and Leila, the geckos, stalked around on the kitchen table while they ate, Howard snapping up bacon crumbs and staring at

Livvie with his yellow eyes. After dessert (hot fudge sundaes), Livvie played a computer game while Peter and Phil talked about comets and meteorites. At nine-fifteen she told them that she was tired, and she went to bed on the couch in the living room.

In the morning, knowing that her mother had gotten to Arizona safely, Livvie felt better. Listening to Phil and Peter walking around the house, she stretched and unzipped her sleeping bag. The bag was lined with pictures of hunting dogs, ducks, and men with guns. Phil had probably bought it at a garage sale.

She made some noise getting dressed so that they would know she was coming, then washed her face and brushed her teeth and went into the kitchen. Thankfully, they were both dressed, though Peter's hair was standing up on his head in little clumps.

"Do you want some breakfast?" Phil asked. "We're making pancakes."

"Sure." Livvie loved pancakes. But it made her nervous to think that the menu had been chosen to please her. "Or whatever's easy. I don't care."

"Pancakes are easy. Re-Pete's already got the batter going. I'm working on fruit."

Livvie glanced at the cutting board by the sink. With toothpicks, Phil was building little edible creatures: pineapple wedges for the feet, a whole peeled kiwi for the body, a circle of orange and two little blueberries for the face and eyes. "Interesting," Livvie said. "Did you just make this up right now?"

"You should see what he can do in the summer with watermelon," Peter said.

Livvie helped herself to juice in a glass. Several minutes later, she sat down to a pancake in the shape of her name. Peter's pancake, a little harder to read, spelled out *Wiseguy*.

"What do you want to do today?" Peter asked.

"I don't know." Livvie shrugged. Her mother had told her to be nice to Peter. Did that mean she was supposed to spend the entire day with him?

Phil poured himself a cup of coffee and said that he had to work, but that Livvie and Peter should feel free to entertain themselves, as long as their idea of fun didn't involve lighter fluid or throwing themselves under a moving train, and as long as they were both back in the house by six p.m.

"I might take the bus to the library," Peter said. He had eaten the *guy* in his pancake and was left with *Wise*.

"Is it open?"

"Sure. Why would they close it?"

Livvie plucked the orange-slice head from the mythical fruit beast Phil had given her. "Maybe I'll go with you. Joyce is probably going to sleep until noon. Do you mind feeding Dr. Brown along the way?"

Peter didn't. After breakfast, Livvie fit another stocking cap over her toes, and they put on their coats and headed out. Peter fastened the bolt on the door with a key.

"You bolt the door when your dad's at home?"

He didn't answer.

"Is it because of the doll-stealing guy?" Livvie asked. "Did the police ever find him?"

"We know who he is." Peter pulled up the hood on his jacket. "I've even seen him walking past our house. His name is Pond."

They started walking slowly to Livvie's. "You'd think a person with a name like *Pond* would be very peaceful," Livvie said. "Why does he walk past your house?"

"I don't know," Peter said. "My dad says as long as he's just walking, it doesn't matter."

At Livvie's they brought in the paper and the mail and poured some more cat food and water into Dr. Brown's plastic dish. "How will we know which bus to take to the library?" Livvie asked.

Peter looked up from the newspaper, which he'd spread across the counter. He was the only sixth grader Livvie knew who read the paper. "You don't know how to take the bus?"

"Well, I know how you get on it," Livvie said. She felt like a jerk. Why hadn't her mother taught her to use the bus? Why did Peter and Joyce know how to do things she had no idea how to do?

"Okay," Peter said. "There are two main buses that are easy to catch from here. One goes east and west on Grand Avenue, and the other goes north and south on Cleveland."

"You mean *down* Cleveland," Livvie said. She pointed in the direction she thought the bus would go.

Peter looked at her steadily. "Which side of the street do you live on, north or south?"

"That depends," Livvie said. "I mean, are you stand-ing in the backyard, or looking at the house from the front?"

Peter pushed his hands deep into his pockets. "Okay. Forget it. Never mind. Just remember that from here the library is south. That's the way you want to go on the bus."

"Okay." Livvie nodded. "And how do we know when we want to get off? I mean, how does the driver know?" She heard a thump from the bedroom: Dr. Brown had probably decided to look for his break-fast.

"Here's what we'll do," Peter said. "We'll go to the library, and then we'll come back and check on the snow maze, because my dad wants to know what's go-ing on up there today, and then we'll take another bus up Grand Avenue—that's east—and buy some egg rolls. I've got my allowance. And you'll get us there. You'll figure out how to do it. But I'll correct you if you're wrong, so we won't get lost."

Livvie folded her arms across her chest. "That's the longest speech I've ever heard you give," she said.

"Very funny." Peter handed her her jacket.

Livvie managed to get them to the library, which was closed. Peter was amazed. "Wouldn't a lot of kids want to come here over the break?"

"No," Livvie said. "If they did, they'd obviously be standing here reading this CLOSED sign with us."

They waited twenty minutes for the return bus,

which let them off in front of Krull's. Livvie was so cold by the time they got there that she ended up going in for hot chocolate while Peter walked across the street to the maze. Ten minutes later, after massaging her toes in the bakery, she hobbled after him with an extra cup of chocolate, spilling about a third of it on her way. "Sorry," she said. "They wouldn't give me a lid. And I asked them nicely."

Peter was checking the sign-up sheet. "I changed our schedules," he said. "So we can work together tomorrow."

Livvie nodded. It would have been lonely walking up to the maze on her own.

Out on the street, cars were slowing down so that the people inside them could look at the maze. There was a sign in front of it that said ST. PAUL SIXTH GRADE FUNDRAISING PROJECT: OPENING JANUARY FIRST. Mr. Gramenz, the computer teacher, was keeping a dozen younger kids away from the entrance.

"I didn't think it would ever be this big," Livvie said. "I'm kind of surprised. Do you think people will really get lost in it?"

"Not permanently." Peter seemed distracted.

"I wish Joyce could see it," Livvie said. "I mean, up close. It's so shiny. I love the way you can almost see through the ice. What are you looking at?"

Peter was staring over her shoulder.

She turned around. "What is it?" She saw two kids wrestling near the edge of the fence, a couple of adults filling wheelbarrows with snow, and a car parked on the street in a no-parking zone. A white van. "What's the matter?"

"I've seen that van before," Peter said.

"So?" Livvie looked more carefully. By squinting at the van she could just get a glimpse of the man inside it. He was thin, with badly cut dark hair, and he was wearing a dark jacket. "Maybe he lives around here."

"No. I think that's him. I mean Pond," Peter said. He started walking, then running, toward the edge of the field. Just when he reached the sidewalk, the van drove off.

Picking her way around a snowbank, Livvie caught up with Peter a few minutes later. She grabbed the collar of his jacket. "Do you mind if I say something?" she asked. "Can I just point out that it is *not* a good idea to run toward a weirdo in a parked car when that weirdo is a person who seems to hate your family?"

"I wasn't sure it was him," Peter said. "I wanted to be sure."

"And now you *are* sure?" Livvie asked. "So what were you going to do—bang on his window?"

"I would have kept my distance," Peter said. "I'm not stupid."

"Then try not to act like it," Livvie told him.

Above them, the sky was thickening and turning gray. Peter was scowling. She had made him angry again. "Let's not talk about it anymore," he said. "Do you still want those egg rolls?"

"No." Livvie was angry, too, though she wasn't sure why. "I don't want any egg rolls."

"Fine, then," Peter said. "I'll see you later." He threw his cup in the trash and started walking home.

Joyce's eyebrows shot straight up into her hair when Livvie told her about the van. "So this is the same guy who's been harassing them on the phone? The guy who wrecked their car?"

"He didn't *wreck* their car," Livvie said. "He just took the dolls' heads." She propped her leg on the bed. She had walked all the way to Joyce's by herself.

"Maybe you shouldn't stay at their house anymore," Joyce said. "If he's really after them."

"I don't think he's *after* them." Livvie shifted uncomfortably in her chair. Joyce had a way of making things seem more dramatic than they were. "Anyway, he wasn't doing anything illegal. Lots of people park and look at the maze."

"Was anything written on the van?" Joyce was dressed, but still in bed. "Something like 'Wilson's Flower Shop' or 'Joe's Plumbing'?"

"I don't think so," Livvie said. "But we only saw one side of it. I guess there could have been something written on the other side."

Joyce took off her glasses and cleaned them. Her blue eye was pale—like a planet, Livvie thought. "You should have written down the license number."

"I didn't think of it," Livvie said, surprised. She tried to bring back into her memory what she had seen, and had the maddening feeling that a picture of the license plate was stored away somewhere in her brain, but folded in half so she couldn't see it. Just like the handwriting on the chain letter.

"Did you see the driver?" Joyce asked. "What did he look like? Do you think you'd recognize him if you saw him again?"

Livvie tried once more to summon up a picture. She remembered the rough white skin, the ragged hair, the dark jacket. Probably half the men in St. Paul fit that description.

Out in the hallway Joyce's brothers were fighting, their heads or elbows thwocking against the wall. Joyce didn't even seem to notice. "I went past the maze today," she said. "My dad took me there on the way to the doctor's."

"What did you think?"

"I wasn't allowed to get out of the car." Joyce sipped at a glass of orange juice. "Have you been inside it?"

Livvie nodded. "Not the whole thing. They have different parts of it blocked off. But it's pretty. The hallways are narrow. You have to walk through it one at a time."

Joyce sighed. "When we drove past it this afternoon, I thought it looked like a palace. I probably would have liked working on it," she said. "Has it been fun?"

"Most of the time," Livvie said. "I only helped with the easy parts. Maybe next week you could sit at the entrance and collect the tickets."

"I doubt it," Joyce said. "They'll probably make me stay in bed forever."

There was a crash in the hall, then a thump and some quiet whimpering.

"I know! You could sit at the entrance with a sign," Livvie said. "Like the one I wore, about the chain letter. Everyone in the city is going to go through that maze."

"I could," Joyce said. She put her drink down on the nightstand. "But it might not be worth it."

"Why not? What about our bad luck? Don't you want it to be over? Don't you want to know who sent us the chain letter?"

"I'm tired of thinking about that stupid letter." Joyce rubbed her eyes. "Do you know what I mean? I just want to go back to school like a regular person and forget the whole thing."

Livvie looked at her cast. It was dirty and spotted. "Do you still believe in bad luck?" she asked.

"Maybe it doesn't matter what I believe," Joyce said.

Livvie lifted the curtain away from the window. It was getting dark. Mrs. Pullman had already offered to drive her home. "Well, wherever our lousy luck has been coming from," she said, "this has to be the end of it. Don't you think? I mean, what else can happen to us?" She thought about her mother in Arizona.

"Shhh," Joyce whispered.

Livvie thought she might be falling asleep. But when she stood up to leave the room, she saw that Joyce's eyes were still open. And that on both hands she had her fingers crossed, two narrow Xs resting on top of the flowered sheet.

Chapter Twelve

Phil made spaghetti and meatballs—another of Livvie's favorites—for dinner on her second night. She tried not to eat too eagerly, but ended up having a large plate of seconds and a small plate of thirds. Phil and Peter both ate a lot, too, Phil serving the meatballs from a bowl that was shaped like a giant pair of dice. Toward the end of the meal, Peter showed them how it was possible to suck a full-length noodle up a straw.

That was the trouble, Livvie thought, with staying overnight in another family's house: You saw and learned things about them that you'd rather not know. Like the fact that Peter talked in his sleep. She'd even heard him singing in the middle of the night, a thin version of "Go Tell Aunt Rhody." Worse, she found out that Phil cracked his knuckles, hard. Sometimes, when he finished with his fingers, he'd take hold of a shoulder or an arm and pull at himself, twisting until something popped. It wasn't a quiet little *crick,* but a horrible, deep, crunching noise, like a troll in a forest, chewing wood.

After dinner they played a card game that Peter and Phil had invented. It was called rules, and it had so many rules, in fact, that Livvie couldn't figure out how to play.

"Six of diamonds is wild," Peter said. He plucked a card from her hand.

"I thought the three was wild."

"It was." Peter didn't look up. "But then it got multiplied by two."

He and Phil explained the game to her again, but by the time Livvie's mother called from Arizona, they had laid her hand down on the table and were playing it without her.

Her mother asked how she was doing.

"Fine," Livvie said. "We're playing cards. Sort of. And we've eaten a lot of red meat." She could feel Peter and Phil trying not to listen in on her conversation. "Was the funeral today?"

"This morning," her mother said. "It was sad. But what funeral wouldn't be? Tomorrow we're going to clean out closets. Is everything okay over at the house? How's Dr. Brown?"

"Still invisible. But his food gets eaten, so he must be all right." Livvie considered telling her mother about the white van, but she wasn't sure Peter had talked to Phil about it yet. "Not much else to report," she said.

She looked at the bulletin board on the side of the refrigerator. It was full of photographs: Peter winning a chess match, Peter winning a geography bee, Peter graduating from kindergarten.

"No news is good news," her mother answered. "Are you still working on the maze?"

"Yup. It's almost finished." Livvie told her mother that she had expected the inside of the structure to be warmer. But the few times she'd walked through the entrance, the silence inside the maze had made it seem even colder. It was like walking from a freezer into an even colder freezer.

"I shouldn't run up a bill here," her mother said. "Do you want to put Phil on? Or is he busy?"

At the bottom of the bulletin board Livvie found a picture of herself and Peter. It had probably been taken a few winters before. They had their arms around each other's shoulders, and they were standing in front of Livvie's house, each of them with icicles tucked inside their upper lips, the points hanging down in front of their mouths like walrus tusks. She pulled out the thumbtack, and the photograph slipped through her fingers and skated across the floor. "Sorry, Mom. What?" She looked for the picture but couldn't find it.

"Is Phil—" her mother started.

"Oh, busy," Livvie said. "That's a yes. The answer is yes."

She saw Phil slap a joker on a ten of clubs.

"All right. Just tell him I said hello, then." Her mother told her to stay warm, then told her she loved her and hung up. When Livvie turned around, Phil was getting up from his chair as if ready to take his turn on the phone. He looked embarrassed.

"Oh, sorry." Livvie put the receiver back in its cradle. "Did you want to talk to her?"

"No, that's all right. Don't worry, it's fine." He straightened his ponytail. Was he blushing? Livvie had never seen a grown man blush.

"She sounded tired, you know, because of the funeral." She looked at Peter but he was studying the cards in his hand, probably figuring out the square root of a queen of clubs.

"I'm sure she's exhausted," Phil said. "And it's getting late. I think I'm going to head upstairs for a while. I have some work to catch up on. Re-Pete's going to beat me, anyway."

"You're winning, though," Peter told him.

"That's how fast the game can change." Phil picked up a couple of newspapers (he seemed to subscribe to at least three a day) and climbed the stairs.

Livvie sat down next to Peter at the kitchen table. "Okay," she said. "Maybe I shouldn't have hung up. You probably think I should have let him talk to her."

Peter was finishing the card game by himself.

"I'm not trying to be mean to him," she whispered. "But there's nothing they needed to talk about."

Peter reshuffled the hearts and diamonds and lay the clubs out in front of him on the table.

Livvie leaned toward him. "Did you know he bought my mother a Christmas present?"

Peter frowned. He was concentrating on his game.

Finally, Livvie snatched up a stack of the cards and sat on them. "You didn't tell your dad about the van, did you?"

"That was a good game you just ruined." Peter held out his hand for the cards.

Livvie didn't give them back. "Are you going to tell him?"

"Not unless there's a reason to." Peter lowered his voice. "We don't know what that guy in the van was doing. And maybe it wasn't even him. I couldn't get a good look."

"You *said* it was him," Livvie whispered. "You were ten feet away."

Peter glanced up the stairs. "I'm not going to bother my dad unless I know that something's really happening," he said. "Besides, I didn't hear you telling your mom about the van."

Livvie opened her mouth and then closed it. Partly, she hadn't told her mother because she'd suspected that it would make her want to talk to Phil.

"And it's probably nothing," Peter said. "Pond doesn't bother us anymore. Have you heard the phone ringing upstairs?"

"No," Livvie said. "But—"

"So there's nothing to worry about. It's fine." Peter

found a new deck of cards in the kitchen drawer and started setting up another round of rules.

Livvie woke up late the next morning wondering whether she should have told Phil about the van. She didn't want to do anything behind Peter's back. Still, she decided that she would definitely have to talk to Phil if she or Peter ever saw Pond again.

There was no one in the kitchen. She looked on the cutting board for fruit or vegetable animals, or food in the shape of her name. Nothing. But she heard noises coming from the attached garage. She opened the door and saw Phil bending over the black-and-white-striped car, its hood now painted a vivid red, and a large gold birdcage fastened to its roof. Inside the cage, on a perch, was a plastic bird.

"What do you think?" he asked. A pair of safety goggles dangled around his neck. "We used a welding torch and some industrial adhesive."

On top of the car, the birdcage looked like a cherry on a dish of ice cream. All along the hood where the dolls' heads had been, Livvie saw bunches of plastic fruit: clusters of grapes, apples, grapefruit, bananas, and pears. She quickly made a silent wish: *Please don't let me ever have to ride in that car again.* "When did you do all this?" she asked.

"I don't sleep very well," Phil said. "Sometimes I get up in the middle of the night and putter around. Re-Pete got up a couple hours ago to help me."

Peter was sitting in the car's backseat, reading an astronomy book with a pencil in his hand.

"Won't the bird fall down while you're driving?" Livvie asked. She was trying to be polite.

"No, he shouldn't." Phil pulled on the cage. "He's wired in there pretty good."

Livvie nodded. She wasn't sure what else to say. She didn't think a car with a birdcage on top of it was any less ridiculous than a car covered with doll heads. "If the glue's still drying, you don't have to drive us to the maze today," she said. "Peter and I can walk."

"You're going to have to walk," Phil said. "I've got a meeting at the bank at three, and another appointment later in the afternoon. I won't be able to work on the maze at all."

"But I signed you up." Peter put down his book and got out of the car.

"Sorry." Phil looked at his watch. "I tell you what: I'll meet you at McGuffy's. I'll treat the two of you to dinner." McGuffy's was around the corner from Krull's, across the street from the snow maze.

"Where's your appointment?" Peter asked.

"I don't know yet." Phil lifted the heavy garage door, and a blast of cold air immediately swept toward them. "I'm going to take the new model here for a spin," he said. "And then I've got some errands to take care of. Do either of you need anything?"

"No, thanks," Livvie said.

"Six-thirty at McGuffy's, then." Phil got in the car,

still wearing the goggles around his neck. "I'll see you there."

Livvie spent the morning playing a computer game and reading through some of the books on Peter's shelf. She and Peter made lunch for themselves, then retreated to their separate corners of the house until three-thirty, when Peter came to tell her that it was almost time to walk to the maze. Livvie yawned and stretched and looked out the window. It had been cloudy all day, and now it looked almost like evening. "The sun's going to go down while we're working," she said. "Why did we sign up for such a late time?"

"It was the only slot left," Peter said. He handed Livvie her gloves and her coat, and he waited while she pulled the pom-pom hat over her toes.

By the time the two of them got to the maze, most people had finished working for the day and gone home. Mrs. Holtz, a third-grade teacher at the sign-in table, told them to pick up two shovels and head for the blue flag inside the maze. "Mr. Edman's in there," she said, clapping her mittened hands together. "He'll tell you what to do."

Even though Livvie had been inside it only two days earlier, the maze had changed. The walls were seven feet high. She walked through the entrance and ran her hands along the blocks of snow. Her breath turned to fog in front of her. "I wish the maze could stay up all year," she said to Peter. "Imagine running through it in the summer."

"I don't think it would last very long." Peter headed down the icy corridor but Livvie stopped him.

"Let me go first," she said. "Can I?"

Peter didn't object, so Livvie started down the bright white path, deciding to go straight instead of taking the first left turn.

"We're going east," Peter said. "Now south." He trudged behind her. Finally, they reached a little snow bench that marked a dead end. The blue flag flapped well ahead of them.

"Hey, it's working," Livvie said happily. "I'm really lost. Do you know where we are?"

Peter sighed and grabbed the sleeve of her jacket. "Think about the drawing," he said. "You saw a part of it." He led her back toward the entrance and made two right turns, easily reaching the flag.

They couldn't find Mr. Edman, but there were two wheelbarrows full of snow at the base of the flag, and Peter assumed that they should use them to make the wall in front of them thicker. The outside walls had been doused with water, which had turned to ice, but the inside had to be fortified with snow. Peter tossed the ends of his scarf behind him and set to work.

Livvie was cold already. She hadn't wrapped her foot up well enough. She patched a crack in the wall with a shovelful of snow and glanced down the frozen corridor that led to the center of the maze. The lady or the tiger, Phil had said. Now that she had already gotten lost inside it, Livvie understood why making a choice in the maze would be frightening. What if your sense of direction wasn't very good? What if you were wrong? She felt dazed by the whiteness on every side. The only thing near them that wasn't white was the sky above, a deep gray-blue.

They used up one wheelbarrow's worth of snow and started on the other. The maze was quiet. "It's kind of creepy in here," Livvie said after a little while. "This is where all the lost people are going to be."

Peter pounded some snow into a hole in the wall with his fist. "My dad says there are going to be lost people everywhere. I think that's the point."

Livvie pushed some snow along the wall with her mitten. "Do you think we should just let them go out together?"

"What?" Peter turned around.

"My mom, I mean, and your dad. It's a lot of work trying to keep them apart. And I feel kind of bad about it sometimes."

"My dad embarrasses you," Peter said.

"That's true." Livvie pulled a clump of ice off her mitten. "You don't feel embarrassed by him? Honestly? By his car?"

"Sometimes," Peter said. "But a lot of parents are embarrassing. I don't think it matters very much."

They worked in silence for a little while, Livvie scraping the snow up the walls with a shovel, and Peter

161

patting it down. "I guess you still think my mom's a slob," she said.

They had used up the snow in the second wheelbarrow. "I wouldn't say she's a slob," Peter said. "She's just—"

"A terrible cook," Livvie interrupted.

Peter didn't disagree. "Your mom's a nice person," he said. "When we were in day care together she used to go to the library for me and bring me books."

"She did? What kind of books?"

"Mostly stories about dinosaurs," Peter said. "That was before I got interested in astronomy."

A man with icicles in his beard came whistling around the corner. "There you are," he said. "I thought you were lost. I'm Robert Edman. We're closing up. Mrs. Holtz and I are ready to call it a night. Can you manage one of these wheelbarrows?"

Peter grabbed one and left the other to Mr. Edman. Snow crunching under their feet, they walked out of the maze. At the exit, Livvie stopped and looked up. The sky was staining itself a deeper blue, the early stars sprinkled across it like glitter.

Mr. Edman asked if they needed a ride home.

"No, thanks," Livvie said. "We live nearby." She and Peter signed out at the desk, and Mrs. Holtz folded the sign-up sheet and hurried toward her car.

Peter looked at his watch. "It's only five-fifteen. I think it's too early to wait at McGuffy's. Do you want to go home?"

"Home. Oh, shoot," Livvie said. "I forgot to go by my house today. I need to feed Dr. Brown." She felt in her pockets for the house key; there it was, on its rock-candy key chain. "Do you mind coming with me? We can watch TV for a while, and then walk back up to McGuffy's."

It was cold, about ten degrees, and getting windy. They started down the sidewalk, their breath trailing behind them like streamers.

Livvie's house was dark. On the front steps she picked up the morning paper and the mail and put her key in the lock. They turned on the lights and walked inside. "Dr. Brown? Here, kitty." As usual, the cat refused to show himself. Having a pet like Dr. Brown, Livvie thought, was like not having a pet at all. Upstairs in the kitchen, she turned on the light and refilled the cat's empty dish with water and kibble. "My mom says if Dr. Brown was a real doctor he'd be a specialist. That's what makes him so hard to find. Maybe he'd be a surgeon or a . . . What are you looking at?"

Peter was standing in the upstairs hallway, staring out the window toward the street. Livvie walked up behind him. Out on the sidewalk, in front of the house, was a dark-haired, skinny-legged man in a leather jacket. Livvie wasn't sure whether he could see them, but he was clearly looking up at the house.

"That isn't him, is it?" she asked.

The man shaded his eyes and looked toward them, as if he had heard her. Peter stumbled away from the window and pulled Livvie with him, nearly knocking her down. "Did you lock the door downstairs when we came in?"

"I don't think I even closed it. Peter, is that him? Lake, or Stream, or whatever?"

"Pond. I don't know. I'll go close the door."

"No!" Livvie grabbed his shoulder. "Look, he's gone. Where did he go?"

"Never mind. We're going out the back," Peter said. "Down the back stairs."

"I can't." Livvie pointed to her leg. "I'll probably fall."

"What about your neighbor? Where's Darryl?" Peter was whispering.

Livvie heard a thump and felt Dr. Brown brush past her. "I don't think he's home yet," she said. Then she remembered. "But we have his key." Peter followed her into the kitchen, turning out lights along the way. In the dark, her hands shaking, Livvie managed to open the kitchen cabinet, pull the key off its peg, and hobble toward the back door. They went out onto the icy back deck, quietly closing the storm door behind them. Livvie put the key into Darryl's lock and pushed her way into his kitchen, which was back to back with their own.

"Stay quiet," Peter whispered. "And leave the lights off." He was holding her hand, clutching it. Or else Livvie was clutching his. "Do you hear anything?"

Livvie stood still and listened. From their own side of the wall, it always seemed as if they could hear Darryl's every movement; they heard his radio, his shower, his phone calls, the creak of his footsteps on the stairs. Now, from Darryl's side, she could hear nothing. "Maybe he's a deliveryman," she said. "Maybe he was just bringing us a package."

"He didn't have a package with him," Peter said.

"Should we call the police?" Livvie tried to imagine what they would say. *We saw a guy on the sidewalk, so we had to break into my neighbor's apartment.* Her mother would be furious. She would think it was just superstition—

"Hello?" The voice seemed to come from right behind them. Livvie squeezed Peter's hand so hard his fingers cracked. She turned around but no one was there.

Peter touched a finger to her mouth, then pointed at a heating vent in the floor. The voice had come through it, from Livvie and her mother's side of the house.

Livvie's heart was slamming around in her chest. Someone—Lake, or Pond, or someone else—had broken into her apartment. Maybe he was stealing something. The silver? Livvie's mother didn't have any silver. The TV or the computer? Neither of them worked very well; they were old. Livvie looked for a phone. Where did Darryl keep his phone? They heard footsteps. The floor creaked. Then they heard a door close.

Peter crawled through Darryl's bedroom to the front window overlooking the street. "There he goes. Look."

Livvie felt her good leg shaking. Slowly, she crept up behind Peter. Out on the street, pulling away, was the white van. Now that she was looking at it, the van clicked back neatly into her memory, as if a lock had turned and let her in. A dent on the right side. A missing back fender. Minnesota license EFX 779. "What was he doing? Was he following us? Why would he follow us?"

Neither of them moved. Livvie's chin was almost touching Peter's shoulder. She recited the license to herself: EFX 779, EFX 779. "He's just some weirdo, some jerk," she said. "He wouldn't actually hurt anybody, would he? Peter?"

Peter turned around. Livvie could feel him thinking. "We'll go to your house and return the key," he said. "Then we'll call my dad."

Chapter Thirteen

They called him. Over and over. Livvie's teeth were clattering together the entire time.

"Something's wrong with the phone," Peter said. "It keeps ringing but the answering machine isn't picking up. I'm going to walk over there." He zipped his jacket.

"What?" Livvie looked outside. It was dark. The branches of the trees were creaking and scratching against the house. "But he isn't going to be there. Didn't he have an appointment?"

Peter put on his gloves. "It might be over already," he said. "I'll call you when I get there."

Livvie just stared at him. Her big toe ached. She didn't want to go back outside; it was windy and she could tell it was getting colder. She didn't even want to look at the thermometer. "I'm going with you. I'm not going to stay here by myself."

Peter looked at her skeptically. But he took off his scarf and wrapped it around her neck. Because her hands were shaking, he even zipped her jacket for her and held out her mittens so that she could put them on.

They took the key with them and locked the door on their way out, Livvie looking up and down the street the entire time.

"Come on." Peter helped her down the front steps as if she were an old lady. The snow was blowing up in tufts around their feet. "Can you make it if we cut through the yards?" He didn't wait for her to answer, but took her arm and led her across the street and between the houses.

Livvie struggled through the snow. Fear, she realized, had taken her breath away and made her tired. "Why don't people shovel their back sidewalks?" she asked. "Don't they know we might need to cut through here?"

They had gone only a hundred yards when she had to sit down on someone's woodpile. Her toe was throbbing and the wind was getting stronger, blowing the snow into little white cyclones across the yards.

Peter looked at his watch. "It's almost quarter to six," he said. "We'll have to start walking to McGuffy's soon."

"Don't even think about leaving me here," Livvie told him, shivering and trying to catch her breath. "Look, why don't we just go to Joyce's? We're practically in her backyard right now, and we can call from there. If you're in too much of a hurry to get back to your dad's you can drop me off."

Peter pulled Livvie to her feet and they cut across the street and through two more side yards to arrive at Joyce's back door, just as a flash of lightning lit up the sky behind them. For the first time in her life, Livvie rang the bell and heard nothing but silence on the other side.

"It's going to storm," Peter said.

Livvie pressed the bell harder. "That's weird. The Pullmans never go out. Not all at one time. They can barely fit in one car." She looked over her shoulder for the white van.

There was another flash of lightning, then a growl of thunder. They were getting ready to give up and head for Peter's when the door opened. Joyce stood in front of them in a pair of gray sweatpants and a pajama top printed with dancing bears. "I'm supposed to be sleeping but someone kept ringing the doorbell," she said. "What's up?"

Peter pushed past her. "Are you here by yourself?"

"Yup. The boys are out bowling with some friends, and my parents went out to dinner for their anniversary. The invalid had to stay behind. I'm eating cereal for dinner and watching the Weather Channel. Did you know there's a low-pressure system heading our way?"

"Joyce, we need to come in," Livvie said.

"Guess what. You *are* in."

This seemed to be true. The door had already closed behind them, and Livvie and Peter were standing in the

Pullmans' kitchen. A rack for coats and boots, about eight feet long, was mostly empty in the hall. Without turning around, Livvie reached behind her and bolted the door. Peter was already heading toward the phone.

"Okay." Joyce looked nervous. "What's going on?"

"Your phone doesn't work," Peter said. He shook the receiver.

"I know," said Joyce. "It's the storm. Some of the lines are down."

"Let's find a phone that works and call the police." Livvie felt sick, as if she had swallowed a glassful of soapy water.

"What are you going to tell them?" Peter asked. "That you saw a van parked on a street? That you heard someone yell hello when you left the door to your house wide open?" He put his hat and gloves on again.

"I don't get it," Joyce said. "Are you talking about the guy in the van? The doll-killer?"

Livvie explained what had happened.

Peter picked up the phone again, then put it down. "I want to find out where my dad went." He frowned. "He should have told me where his appointment was. That isn't like him."

"What isn't like him?" Joyce asked. "We're talking about a man who drives a car covered with doll heads."

"No," Livvie said. She was still shivering. "He's got a birdcage now."

A clap of thunder crashed over the house. The lights dimmed for a moment, then brightened again.

Peter headed for the door, but Joyce pulled him

back, grabbing his collar. "Hold on. We're going with you."

Livvie stared at her. "Joyce? You're wearing pajamas."

Joyce picked up a sweater from the back of a chair and put it on. "Now I'm not."

"But aren't you supposed to stay in bed?"

"You got me out of bed, didn't you? And if you think I'm staying here by myself after you barged in here to tell me a creepy story . . . well, forget it." She pulled on a pair of boots, then a hat and gloves. She turned to Peter. "We'll go look for your dad at your house. If he isn't there, we'll go to McGuffy's. We'll stick together. All right?"

Peter seemed about to argue, but he agreed.

Joyce put on her coat and looked through the peephole in the door. "Coast is clear," she said. "Let's go."

The air stung Livvie's eyes and hurt her nose. She breathed through a mitten, one hand cupped against her face. Peter walked in front of them, cutting a path through the falling snow. On the back of his jacket was a small reflective orange triangle. Livvie kept her eyes on it. Joyce shouted something in her direction, but the words disappeared immediately in the storm.

None of the lights were on in Peter's house when they got there. The mannequins in the front yard smiled at them from a snowdrift. "Move over, lady," Joyce said, shoving the female mannequin aside.

Peter put the key into the lock, pushed the door open, and turned on the lights. "Dad?"

No answer.

"Phil?" Livvie called.

Joyce shut the door behind them. "Mr. Finch?"

Peter switched on the lights in the living room and the kitchen. Everything looked the same—untouched. There was a coffee cup in the sink. "He must have come home," Peter said, looking at the cup.

Howard and Leila were basking in the glare of their heat lamp.

"Maybe he left you a note somewhere," Joyce said. She looked through a stack of school flyers on the kitchen table.

Peter picked up the phone. "It's dead." He chewed his thumbnail. Then he looked up the circular stairs toward his father's study.

"Your dad won't mind us going up there if it's an emergency," Joyce said.

The wind was getting louder.

"Are any of your neighbors home?" Livvie asked. She didn't like the way the upstairs looked so dark.

Peter opened the door between the kitchen and the garage. "The car is gone," he said, still chewing his nail. "I'll just go up and look at his calendar." He nodded to Livvie and Joyce. "You two stay here."

Livvie wasn't sure whether they'd agreed to stay behind or not, but as soon as Peter started up the steps, they were right behind him, nearly stepping on his heels.

"It's cold up here," Joyce said, putting her hand on the metal banister. "Why is it so cold?"

Peter was stumbling ahead of them, searching for the light.

"It feels like there's a window open," Livvie said, holding Joyce's hand. "Or like there's a—"

Peter switched on the light.

"Hole in the ceiling," Joyce finished.

The three of them looked up. It wasn't just a hole in the ceiling. It was a hole that went right through the roof. It was big—about three square feet—and it was thinly covered with a sheet of plastic.

"Peter," Livvie said. "Your house has a hole in it. Is that what your dad didn't want us to see?"

Peter didn't answer. He wasn't even looking at the hole. He was looking at something in the corner of the study, past the exercise bike, the yellow couch, and the mess of papers on the floor. "I don't believe it," he said.

"Believe what?" Joyce asked. "What is that?"

"Is it a telescope?" Livvie asked.

"No. It's not a telescope." Peter was wide-eyed. "It's a ten-inch reflector telescope. With computer tracking. You can track the movement of planets and comets and stars. I've wanted one of these forever."

"He must have bought it for your birthday." Livvie shook her head. "January third. That's why he didn't want us coming up here." She felt a flush of shame, remembering what she had said to Joyce about Phil hiding something up in his study. "I guess it was supposed to be a surprise."

Peter was hovering by the telescope but hadn't touched it. He seemed to be afraid to. "You can hook this up to the computer," he said, his voice just above a whisper. "And with that hole in the roof—"

"Hey, Peter?" Joyce was standing at the desk. "I think I found his calendar."

Peter seemed to tear himself away from the telescope. All three of them looked at the leather binder that lay open in the center of his father's desk. Next to the day's date was a scribbled notation: *5:00*. And on the same page, just below it, was a plastic toy, the figure of an animal. A tiger.

The plastic that covered the hole in the ceiling started flapping. Livvie jumped.

Peter picked up the tiger. "I think we should go now," he said.

"I don't want to leave," Livvie almost whimpered. "Phil might come back here to look for us. Shouldn't we wait for him?"

"No way," Joyce said. "The phones aren't working, and I still have a giant case of the creeps. We'll tell him where we are." She found a pencil and paper and wrote, *Hey, Phil. Went to McGuffy's. 6:15. There are three of us.* "He might be waiting for us up there already," she said. "I mean, waiting for you." She started downstairs. Peter and Livvie followed her, Peter slipping the little plastic tiger into his pocket. They left the note on the kitchen table, turned the lights off when they left, and locked the door.

On the way to McGuffy's, Peter speed-walked ahead while Livvie and Joyce both struggled behind. Every few minutes he turned around and waited for them, managing to look impatient even though his face was well wrapped up.

Joyce shouted something in Livvie's ear.

"What?" Livvie was looking for the white van. If she saw it she was going to grab hold of Joyce and drag her to the first house they could find that had a light on, and she would pound on the door and yell until someone answered.

She looked for the orange triangle on Peter's jacket and followed it. The snow was falling in every direction, and it was getting difficult to tell where the sidewalk was.

By the time they opened the door to McGuffy's, Joyce's glasses were coated with ice. Phil wasn't there. Only two of the red vinyl booths were taken, one by a family with a little girl, and the other by two high school boys who had ordered several hamburgers each. It was probably too cold for everyone else.

"Maybe the storm slowed him down," Livvie said. "We know he's driving." They sat in the corner by the window, which gave them a good view of the intersection as well as the maze. They would be able to see Phil coming from any direction.

"Thanks for letting me tag along, you guys," Joyce said. "I'm pretty hungry."

"Just don't eat off my plate," Livvie told her. She was happy to be in a well-lit place, with other people. "And don't dip your fries into my ketchup. I don't want to get sick."

"I think it's too late for you to get sick. At least from me. I'm not contagious anymore." Joyce picked up a menu. "How much money do you have?"

The windows were all fogged up. Peter used his sleeve to wipe the condensation off the glass.

"Money?" Livvie put her hands into her pockets. She had one wrinkled dollar and a little change. "I thought you had money. You always have money. I haven't gotten my allowance."

Joyce had forty-seven cents in her jacket pocket. And she found a quarter in her mother's sweater. After the waitress brought them three cups of water and went back to the kitchen, Joyce stood up and lifted the red vinyl cushion on her seat.

"What are you doing?" Livvie asked.

Joyce knelt on the sticky linoleum floor. "Jackpot!" Beneath the seat cushion, she found a quarter, two dimes, and several pennies, which she dumped on the table. Still looking out the window, Peter added a handful of change.

"Excellent," Joyce said, sitting back down. "We can get french fries. And a big chocolate malt."

Livvie put all their money in a little pile and added up

the prices by counting on her fingers. They would have seven cents left for a tip.

The waitress came over and took their order, glancing suspiciously at the heap of coins. When the waitress headed back toward the kitchen, Joyce elbowed Livvie in the ribs and nodded at Peter, who was tapping a finger against his forehead.

"Your dad'll show up," Joyce said. "He's not very late yet."

Livvie agreed. She was thinking about the telescope and the hole in Phil's roof. She doubted there were many parents who would cut a hole in the top of their house for a birthday present.

Joyce spun a quarter on the tabletop. "Phil was probably here, and when the two of you didn't show up, he went off to look for you. As soon as he finds that note he'll come right back. Then we can ask him what else he's buying you for your birthday."

"Joyce!" Livvie said.

"I'm only kidding. Jeez. Sitting here worrying isn't going to do us any good."

The family with the little girl paid the waitress and left.

"You're the one who usually worries," Livvie told Joyce. "All that banging on streetlights and knocking on wood—"

Peter took the plastic tiger out of his pocket and set it on the table.

"Touching the streetlights isn't worrying," Joyce

said. "Anyway, I might give all that stuff up." She sipped her water and leaned back in the booth.

"No more avoiding the cracks in the sidewalk?" Livvie asked. "No more twirling the knobs on the lockers?"

"We'll be graduating sixth grade this spring, Livvie. Things are going to be different in junior high."

"Different how?"

The waitress arrived with their french fries, and Joyce immediately flooded them with ketchup. The sleeves of her sweater were too short; her pajama top was showing at the wrists. "We'll be older," she said. "We'll have to act older. We'll try different things. You know—the world is our oyster and all of that."

"I don't like oysters," Livvie said.

The high school boys had finished their mountain of food and left their table. Looking irritable, the waitress poured a chocolate malt into three separate cups and announced that the restaurant was closing early. "Because of the storm," she said. "I don't think anybody else is coming."

Peter stood up and walked off toward the bathroom without saying a word.

"It does seem strange that Phil isn't here yet," Livvie told Joyce. "Shouldn't he have seen your note by now?"

They looked out the window. Around the globe of the streetlight, snowflakes were circling, like moths in summer. The snow maze, across the street, seemed to crouch like an animal in the dark.

"He'll see it." Joyce yawned. She set her glasses on the table, made a pillow out of her down jacket, and closed her eyes.

"You aren't falling asleep, are you?" Livvie asked.

"No." Joyce put another french fry in her mouth, but took a very long time to chew it.

"Joyce, you can't fall asleep. You have to help me think of what to do."

The waitress was clanking dishes together in the kitchen behind them.

"Joyce?"

"Nice-looking rabbit," Joyce murmured. Her blue eye fluttered. She began to snore.

Livvie scraped some ketchup off the french fries and ate them. It was thoroughly dark outside, and she began to wonder where she and Peter and Joyce were supposed to go if Phil didn't show up very soon.

Peter came back from the bathroom and sat down but didn't say anything. Livvie watched him pick up the little tiger and study it, staring into its beady plastic eyes.

"He must have had it up there in his study because of the maze," she said. "You know, the lady or the tiger."

"Uhn," Peter said. Livvie could tell he was thinking; he didn't like to talk when he was thinking.

She sorted the coins on the table into little rows, the quarters in one row, the dimes in another. She was lining up the nickels and wondering how they were going to explain their situation to the waitress when, out the corner of her eye, she saw someone pull up in front of the maze across the street.

She squinted, then shivered. "Um, Peter?"

"I knew he'd get here," Peter said, the little tiger tumbling out of his hand and across the row of coins. "He was probably just—" Then he looked out the window and saw the van. A man in a short dark jacket had gotten out of the driver's side and slammed the door.

"What's he doing here?" Livvie asked. "And where's Phil?" She reached out to take hold of Peter's sleeve, but he backed away. His feet didn't seem to touch the ground on his way out the door.

"Peter!" Livvie grabbed Joyce by the neck of her sweater and nearly dragged her from the booth.

"I can't swim that far," Joyce muttered. Her eyes were still closed.

Livvie shook her. She picked up their jackets, wrapping both of them around Joyce's shoulders. She held a scarf in front of Joyce's face and pulled her into the storm.

Across the street, through the blowing snow, they saw Peter rounding the fence at the edge of the baseball field. Pond was nowhere in sight.

"Peter, wait!" Livvie shouted. But the wind lifted her voice and carried it away.

Peter didn't look back. The last thing Livvie saw before he disappeared around the corner of the maze was the reflective marker on his jacket, a bright orange triangle flashing in the gusting snow.

Chapter Fourteen

"*Did you see* where he went?" Livvie shouted. "Joyce, weren't you watching?"

She turned and saw that Joyce didn't have her glasses on. She must have left them in the restaurant.

"Do you think they went in the maze?" Joyce shouted back. She looked exhausted, as if she was about to fall over.

"You go back inside," Livvie told her. "Call the police. Talk to the waitress. Tell her what happened. I'm going to wait here." She turned back to the maze, wondering what was going on inside it.

"Livvie?" Joyce was breathing hard. "I don't like the way things are turning out here. I think you should come back to the restaurant with me."

"One of us has to watch for Peter," Livvie said. "Don't worry, I'll stay right here. Now hurry up. Go."

Joyce stumbled off, Livvie gradually losing sight of her in the whirling snow.

"Peter?" Livvie yelled. Behind her, the van was still parked beneath a streetlamp. Was Phil supposed to be meeting Pond inside the maze? Was that what the plastic tiger meant? But if Phil was in the maze, where was his car?

Clumsily, Livvie walked across the street, around the fence, and across the first-base line. There was no sign of Peter. Ten yards away, the entrance to the maze was an open mouth.

There was no one on the baseball field. No dog walkers, no evening joggers. It was so cold; she was an idiot to have forgotten to get her jacket from Joyce.

Livvie took one step, then two toward the maze's entrance. She counted up her episodes of bad luck. Plenty of lousy things had happened to both her and Joyce, and now bad luck had also struck Livvie's mother. Livvie felt dread swelling inside her like a balloon. Nothing bad had happened to Phil or Peter—at least not yet.

"Hello?" She took a few more steps. A few more. She was in the maze.

Without really seeing them, Livvie remembered the first two turns, avoiding the dead end, like an icy pocket, that she and Peter had stumbled into. *North, south, east, west.* She had never been in the maze after dark, and her mother was right: She was the worst person in the world at finding her way. She tried to orient herself, but the blue flag was gone, and the wind was blowing in all directions. Overhead, there was no moon; the sky was a wet gray lid above the walls.

She stopped to rub her arms and legs, then turned another corner. This was Joyce's blurry version of the world, except that Livvie couldn't put on a pair of glasses to make it clearer. Somewhere ahead of her in the darkness, she heard something fall. "Peter?"

She pulled her hands into the sleeves of her sweatshirt. Joyce would be back with a police car soon.

In the hazy darkness, Livvie felt a blast of cold air coming in from her left; she must have passed by the entrance again. She turned around and tried to retrace her steps. She had completely lost track of where she was.

Livvie tried not to panic. What did her mother always tell her when she was nervous or afraid? *Keep calm. Think. Try to use your head.* She took a deep breath, then chose a path to her right. What would she do if she found Pond instead of Peter? There was another noise behind her. She strained her eyes against the dark but couldn't see.

She had several choices. She could stay where she was and shout, hoping that the police (but not Pond) would come and find her. She could try to feel her way back to the entrance to look for Joyce. Or she could keep pushing her way through the maze to make sure that nothing had happened to Peter. She wanted magically to be at home with her mother, and with Dr. Brown, watching a video with her leg propped on a chair.

The important thing, Livvie knew, was to try to keep moving. She wiped her nose on her sleeve and thought about frostbite, about people whose toes had to be amputated from the cold. Her feet were numb, but she could still move them. And she could keep her fingers warm inside her shirt. She stopped to rub the feeling back into her ears, then carefully navigated another passage. If Peter had found the doll-killer, she probably would have heard him. He would have shouted— wouldn't he?—for help.

Livvie turned another corner. The maze seemed enormous. She held out her arms and realized she was standing at a sort of crossroads. She had reached it, the point in Phil's drawing: *the lady or the tiger.*

Livvie rubbed her arms and blew on her hands and studied the three paths in front of her, like three open doors. She stood still, her breath steaming.

She remembered what Phil had said about people not wanting to make decisions. They wanted someone else to make their choices for them. But Livvie had already made a choice: She had entered the maze. And before that she had broken her toe because she had *chosen* to take out the trash. She had also *chosen* to try to keep her mother and Phil apart.

All of her life, she'd been making choices. But there were some things you could control and some you couldn't, her mother had said. Maybe her mother was right. Maybe all you could do was try to think clearly, then pick and move forward.

"Peter?" she whispered. She rubbed her frozen hands together. Eenie-meenie-minie-moe.

The middle of the three paths zigzagged left, then right. Livvie couldn't see her own feet in the darkness. *Think. Think,* she told herself. If the path led her back to the entrance, she would circle the maze and look for Joyce. If it led her to the exit, she would do the same thing. Peter had probably found his way out already. All she had to do was walk through the icy corridors carefully, and she would be back in civilization soon.

Except that her hands were reaching out and finding nothing but ice. There was a wall to her left, and a wall in front of her. She pushed her fists out of her sleeves to make sure. She had reached a dead end.

Livvie felt the tears well up in her eyes. The cold seemed to enter her skeleton through her clothes. She wanted her jacket. She wanted a hot chocolate. Though it was difficult with the cast on her leg, she knelt down on the ground. Maybe there was a hole in the wall, or a tunnel. Maybe she could dig her way out with a rock. But there were no rocks, and no tunnels: There was only a little bench made of ice.

She was about to make her way back to the center of the maze when she heard a scrape and a grunt, as if a knee or elbow had crunched against the wall. "Peter?" Nothing but silence at first, and then she heard footsteps. She backed up slowly, on her hands and knees.

Someone was groping his way along the passage. Was it the doll-killer? She crawled back to the ice bench and curled up into a ball beside it. Her hands were numb; she tucked them into her armpits to get warm.

Whoever was walking through the maze had stopped. Maybe he was listening. *Quiet,* she thought. Her heart was pounding. *Keep calm.*

Phil would show up at McGuffy's soon. He would have seen the note in the kitchen, and Joyce would tell him to look for Livvie in the maze. He would come and find her. Of course he would. She wished she had treated him as well as he deserved.

The lady or the tiger, the lady or the tiger. It was hard to make the right decisions, hard to trust yourself. She looked at the starless sky and shivered. She closed her eyes.

The flashlights moving toward her looked like something from a dream. They looked like fireflies, but bigger. They were bobbing up and down in the dark, and they were talking to her, excited, some of them calling to her by name. *Livvie,* they said. *Here you are. We found you.* Then one of the fireflies, the largest and brightest, landed squarely on her knee. *Re-Liv,* it said. *You were trying to find us. Is that why you're here?* It took her a moment to respond; parts of her seemed to be asleep. She sat up stiffly and shivered, and someone wrapped a heavy cloth around her. Maybe part of a cocoon, Livvie thought. Did fireflies weave cocoons?

With the other flashlights still bobbing and dancing around her, she felt herself wrapped up and lifted. She was carried out of the maze and driven home.

Even though Phil turned the heat inside the house up to eighty-two and wrapped her in blankets and sat her in front of the radiator, Livvie was still cold. He gave her hot chocolate and insisted that she take a bath.

Joyce helped her. The phones were working again, so she had left a message for her parents and then filled the tub with hot water and bubbles. "Phil didn't have bubble bath," she told Livvie. "So I used laundry soap."

Livvie didn't care. The hot water hurt and felt good, as if her skin were being raked with a thousand needles. She lay back in the tub very slowly, her cast draped awkwardly over the side.

"You were out there a long time," Joyce said. She sat on the bathroom floor, talking to Livvie through the shower curtain, on which was printed a map of the world. Livvie could see Joyce's head behind Australia. "It was like you disappeared or something. I thought you'd been kidnapped." Joyce had staggered back to McGuffy's but the phone there didn't work. So she had walked several blocks to a pay phone, called the police, and gotten back to McGuffy's in time to see Phil and Peter talking to two uniformed officers outside the maze. Pond was already in the back of the police car.

"Is Livvie with you?" they had all asked each other.

Livvie propped a washcloth behind her neck as a pillow. "So they really arrested him?" she asked.

"Yup. He was supposed to meet with Phil somewhere at five, but he didn't show up. Are you still shivering?"

"Not really." Livvie wanted to tell Joyce what it was like to be in the maze when it was dark, and to have to make up her mind by herself, to have to choose. "So he and Phil didn't have an appointment to meet at the maze?" she asked.

"Nope. Phil only found out that Pond was there when he heard it from Peter." Joyce laughed. "You know, even Re-Pete got lost in there for a while. He swore his dad changed the drawings."

Livvie folded a second washcloth and put it behind her knee. She didn't want her cast getting wet.

"Phil thinks Pond was going to wreck the maze. He says they can get him for vandalism, and maybe also for stalking," Joyce said. "He's going to talk to a lawyer."

Livvie wiped some bubbles off the shower curtain, near Argentina. She didn't want to think about Pond for a while—not yet. "I think my foot's falling asleep," she said.

"Time to get out, then." Joyce pushed herself off the floor and held out a towel. "I feel bad for Phil. His car stalled out for a while on his way back, and he was trying to call us. You should have seen him; he was really worried."

The tub was hard to get out of. It was one of those old-fashioned kinds, a deep old claw-foot. Livvie grabbed Joyce's elbow.

"Jeez, you're slippery." Joyce struggled with her from behind the curtain. "You're like a fish. Did you rinse off the soap?"

"It's okay; I'm up," Livvie said. She put her cast on the tile floor and grabbed for the towel. "Thanks, Joyce."

"Don't mention it." Joyce sat down on the lid of the toilet. "What are friends for?"

Livvie took a long time getting dressed. She wrapped a towel around her hair and then called her mother in Arizona. It was hard to explain exactly what had happened; she had to tell the entire story twice.

"I'm still not sure I understand you," her mother said. Livvie could picture her clutching the receiver. "This man was following you and Peter? Did Phil know he was doing it?"

"We didn't tell him," Livvie said. She was standing in the hall outside the kitchen. "We should have, and we were going to, but it was confusing. And then it was too late. Oh, and I forgot. Phil put a hole in his roof for a telescope."

"A what? I'm sorry, Livvie, I—"

"Never mind," Livvie said. "I'll explain it later. A lot of things have been happening."

"Well, I'm glad you're all right," her mother said. "It all sounds very frightening."

"It was." Livvie thought about the flashlights bobbing toward her in the dark. "I think he saved me," she said. "Phil did."

Her mother was quiet for a moment. "You used your head," she told Livvie. "And you're fortunate to have such loyal friends. Tell Phil I said thank you. And maybe you should tell him . . ." She paused.

On the floor at Livvie's feet, almost hidden beneath the door of a closet, was a slip of paper. Livvie coaxed it from its hiding place with her toe. It was the picture of her and Peter, arms around each other, icicle walrus tusks protruding from their mouths. "Tell him what?" she asked, picking up the photograph.

"Never mind," her mother said. "I'm just glad you're safe." She told Livvie that she would see her in a couple of days, and they hung up.

In the kitchen, Phil was baking bread, and Joyce and Peter were playing checkers.

"Feeling better?" Phil asked. He had flour all over his shirt and up and down his arms.

"I think so." Livvie took the towel off her hair. She was still holding the photograph. She couldn't seem to put it down.

"I remember that picture," Peter said, looking over her shoulder. "We were standing in front of your house, and your mom burned our lunch. King me," he said to Joyce.

Livvie studied the picture. There was something about it, something about the mailbox in the background, or about the writing on it. . . . She sat down with a thump. "I know who sent us the chain letter."

Joyce whirled around in her seat, knocking half the checkers out of their red and black squares. "You do not. Do you?"

"I thought you didn't care anymore," Peter told her.

"Maybe I don't care *as much,*" Joyce said. "But I can still be curious. Can't I? Okay, I'm very curious. Livvie, tell me!"

Livvie kept staring at the photograph. How could she not have seen it earlier? "Darryl," she said. "My neighbor, Darryl."

Joyce's mouth fell open. "Firefighter Darryl? Darryl who pounds on your wall to make you be quiet? Why would he send us a chain letter?"

"I don't know." Livvie held up the picture. "But this is his handwriting. It's on our mailbox." On a large piece of cardboard in his odd, squat cursive, Darryl had written, *Darryl Wright, Kate McFee, Olivia McFee.* He'd had the cardboard laminated, and he'd glued it to the box. There it was in the photo, behind their heads.

"Darryl. I can't believe it." Reaching for the picture, Joyce bumped the checkerboard again, sending the plastic pieces skidding across it. "But why the heck would he send us a chain letter?"

"Probably because he has a granddaughter," Phil said. "She lives in Chicago, and I think she's about your age. She must have given him a copy."

Peter sighed and dumped the checkers back into the box. "Do you think your mom knew that it was Darryl?"

"No. Anyway, I wasn't talking to her about the letter. We were talking about other stuff."

"What other stuff were the two of you talking about?" Phil asked.

Livvie watched him punching the bread dough. He always looked happy when he cooked. He was cheerful and funny and smart, and a good person. "I think she'd probably like to go out with you," she said.

At the kitchen table, Peter and Joyce seemed to turn into statues.

Livvie took a deep breath. "You've always been nice to her," she said. "I mean, to us. It shouldn't matter that you're neat and she's messy, or that you like to cook and she doesn't, or that she likes detective books and you only read history and science. I gave her the earrings. They look really good on her."

"Earrings," Phil repeated. His hands had stopped moving in the dough.

"The ones you gave her for Christmas," Livvie said. "In the little gold box."

"Aha."

"I helped you pick them out. Sort of." Her hair was dripping onto her shoulders. "We went to the store to-gether, remember?"

"I remember that," Phil said. "The little blue earrings. They were for you."

"*What?*"

"Oops," Joyce said. She pinned the photograph back on the bulletin board. "Very big oops."

Livvie stared at Phil. "Me? But why would you buy *me* earrings?"

"Well, I suppose there were several reasons," he said. "I felt bad about your broken toe. And I felt bad about refusing to show you the maze. I thought you ran out of the kitchen that night because I wouldn't show you my drawing. The fact that you fell down the stairs seemed like partly my fault."

"Oh," Livvie said. The kitchen was quiet. She could hear the clock ticking. "You never wanted to ask my mother out?"

Phil scraped a piece of bread dough off his shirt.

"But what about the love letter?" Joyce asked. "With the little hearts around her name?"

"Little hearts?" Phil looked confused.

"Hold on." Peter ran down the hall to his bedroom and came back with the slip of paper. He must have been saving it. *Kate McFee,* it said, the name ringed with hearts.

"Oh, *that*. That was for Valentine's Day." Phil looked at the wrinkled piece of paper. "I was trying to get parents to volunteer for activities at the recreation center. I asked her to organize a Valentine's Day dance for sixth graders but then it turned out we couldn't use the gym."

Livvie slumped down in her chair. No one spoke.

Finally, Joyce tapped Peter on the shoulder. "I think Livvie's going to have to kill you now," she said.

"Actually, I *did* consider asking Kate to go to dinner." Phil was rolling the dough into a sticky white ball with his hands. "But I wasn't sure she would like the idea. And I wasn't sure Re-Liv or Re-Pete would like it, either."

Livvie stared down at her lap for a long moment. Then she looked up at Phil. His top teeth, she thought, weren't as bad as the ones on the bottom. "I didn't like the idea," she said. "But now I think it's probably okay. I've changed my mind."

"Compared to some of the other wackos her mother has gone out with," Joyce said, "you'd probably be— Ow!"

Peter had stepped on her foot. "It's okay with me, also," he said.

Phil divided the bread dough in half and put it into two pans. "Well, it's good to know that I have the approval of Peter Finch and his friend Olivia McFee," he said. "Despite the fact that I have a birdcage on my car."

"And a hole in your roof," Joyce added. She and Peter were setting up another game of checkers.

Phil put the bread pans into the oven. "Thanks for looking for Pete," he told Livvie. "Out there in the maze."

"Thanks for finding me," Livvie answered. She helped Phil clear the dishes. "I can wash these if you want. I'm sure you have other things to do."

"Like what?" Phil smiled. "What else should I be doing?"

Livvie picked up the phone. She dialed her mother's number in Arizona.

Phil hesitated when she handed him the receiver.

"Go ahead," Livvie told him. She had made up her mind and done what she could. The rest was out of her hands. She would have to leave it to Phil and her mother. Or to luck.

About the Author

Julie Schumacher is the author of numerous short stories and two books for adults, including *The Body Is Water*, an Ernest Hemingway Foundation/PEN Award Finalist for First Fiction and an ALA Notable Book of the Year. Delacorte Press published her first novel for young readers, *Grass Angel*.

An associate professor of English at the University of Minnesota, Julie Schumacher lives with her husband and their two daughters in St. Paul.